Praise for *The Risk of Us*

"Rachel Howard has given us a portrait of family-building and attachment that is at once beautiful and painful, serious and funny, page-turning and insightful. I was deeply moved by this novel, a powerful reminder of the risks we take on whenever we love anyone."

— Belle Boggs, author of *The Art of Waiting*

"*The Risk of Us* is a spare, poetic, and fearless narrative that explores the question of what makes — and keeps — a family together. Be prepared for an absorbing, unflinching chronicle of the formidable difficulties and vast rewards of love."
— Krys Lee, author of *How I Became a North Korean* and *Drifting House*

"Howard works with an elegant complexity, rendering family life with its necessary cocktail of pain and humor and pathos. She's the kind of writer I admire most: an unflinching, savage, and ultimately tender eye trying to make sense of all our confusions."
— Joshua Mohr, author of *Termite Parade*

"Rachel Howard's *The Risk of Us* (so accurately titled) is a novel of deep pain yet also laughs — lots of them. Nothing is easy in this book, and that's as it should be. With risk comes a kind of awesome grace. A wonderfully written and candid examination of what it means to be a family."
— Peter Orner, author of *Last Car Over the Sagamore Bridge* and *Love and Shame and Love*

"I've never read anything so beautiful about the intricacies of adoption — the process itself and the seldom-talked-about aftermath. The prose is elegant and compressed; I often had to stop reading to catch my breath. Anyone who has ever loved a child, in any capacity, should read this book."
— Jamie Quatro, author of *I Want to Show You More* and *Fire Sermon*

"This book reads like a thriller. A beautiful story about connection and love despite and beyond trauma."
— Julia Scheeres, author of *Jesus Land*

ALSO BY RACHEL HOWARD

The Lost Night:
A Daughter's Search for the Truth of Her Father's Murder

The
Risk
of Us

RACHEL HOWARD

Houghton Mifflin Harcourt
Boston   New York   2019

hmhco.com

Library of Congress Cataloging-in-Publication Data
Names: Howard, Rachel, 1976– author.
Title: The risk of us / Rachel Howard.
Description: Boston : Houghton Mifflin Harcourt, 2019. |
Includes bibliographical references.
Identifiers: LCCN 2018035807 (print) | LCCN 2018052045 (ebook) |
ISBN 9781328587619 (ebook) | ISBN 9781328588821 (hardcover)
Classification: LCC PS3608.O929 (ebook) | LCC PS3608.O929 R57 2019 (print) |
DDC 813/.6 — dc23
LC record available at https://lccn.loc.gov/2018035807

Book design by Emily Snyder

Printed in the United States of America
DOC 10 9 8 7 6 5 4 3 2 1

To D. and T.

My loves, my life's fulfillment.

One

It starts with a face in a binder. children available, reads the cover. The recruitment brochure for this foster services agency says they need families that "take risks," but I won't notice this language until it's too late, and even if I'd noticed it at the start, I would have taken it as a pat on the back. You, though, you see everything as a warning. You scrutinize the flyers in the binder, search the faces for signs. Read between the lines.

"He looks sweet," I say. "A boy like that, I think we could help him."

"Sexual abuse," you say. "How would he ever trust me?" Turn the page.

The pictures remind me of the advertisements for abandoned dogs in the shelter where I volunteered, back in another life.

Older than seven we've deemed untenable, which means every teenager's smile punctures any temptation to feel virtuous. "It's so unfair, the older ones don't have a chance," I say.

"It's awful," you say. You mean it. You've turned pale. Your bleeding heart, literally and figuratively. It weakens you several times daily. The reason I married you.

"We want the child to have a chance of bonding with us," you say. It's an apology, not an explanation. We've been over this too many times. You made a chart: *Name. DOB. County. Positives. Concerns.* You stop on an Asian girl with big glasses. I read: *Alice would like to be placed with a family that eats organic produce.*

"I like that. She looks smart, that Alice." You're trying out her name. But Alice is nine. So we turn.

To a brown-haired gremlin with arms flung like she could fly off the page.

"Ma-REE-sa?" we say. "Ma-RESS-a?"

The girl beside her has the same brown eyes and brown hair. But she's composed. Forgettable. Or is that just the year and a half since we saw her photo, as I write this, erasing incipient love?

Jennifer and Maresa are adorable eight- and six-year-old sisters. They love dance class, singing, and making art.

Your mouth puckering in thought. "The agency said we can have two of the same sex in one room." My pulse rising at what you don't say: The older girl is eight.

Names and dates of birth at the top of the list, slip of paper handed to the receptionist.

In your handwriting, a special note: *Highly interested.*

You may be the careful one, but you've got your risky side. Saying "I love you" back when I blurted it after three weeks. Following me from San Francisco to North Carolina after three months. Marrying me there after six. Supporting me when I wanted to quit the only college teaching job I'd ever managed to land and go back to California. Signing a mortgage on a house in the foothills, praying our freelance gigs would keep coming even though we'd be hours up Route 80 from the bay, because how else could we ever afford that second bedroom?

The difference with you: You know the risks are real. Whereas I can't quite conjure danger. Blithe, some might say.

You prefer to say I have an optimistic imagination.

Failure of imagination might apply, too. Not long after we write the unpronounceable name, I go for a beer with another writer, rare creature in our new GMC-driving, flag-flying town. You commended me for networking, but what I want in this alien land of live oaks and ponderosa pines is a friend. His perfect baby is home sleeping with his wife. I talk the whole time about the girls in the binder, about waiting to hear. Try not to burden him with details of a labyrinthine bureaucracy, just say we've been specially chosen as a home offering "permanency," though finalizing can't be guaranteed. He applauds what we're doing. Says it sounds risky.

"Maybe this isn't the kind of question I should ask," he starts, "but what happens if — you know — you don't click?"

I explain how the first meetings will go, how the girls supposedly won't know — though how could they not? — that we're scouting.

"I mean beyond that," he says, and I brace myself with another sip of beer. "Not to be callous here, but technically you'll still be foster parents until the final adoption, right? So . . ."

"Oh," I say. "Well . . . we're supposed to be offering unconditional love."

Meaning, *I'm not even going to imagine what you're suggesting.*

C⁓

The week after we hand the names to the receptionist, we drive down to the city. Oh, elaborate life riggings of the so-called creative class. You've kept your adjunct job near the bay, teaching art where we can't afford to live, renting a basement two nights a week from a friend. Oh, fleeting freedom of the childless freelancer. On a whim I join you for the commute. Heading to my old haunt, the cathedral on the hill, while you ride transit to your college. Oh, refuge of my angst-filled twenties. Echoing footfalls, aftertaste of incense. Kneeling for Wednesday-morning prayer with three strangers and the priest who, fifteen years ago, sprinkled water on my forehead. Wandering to the south side-chapel as the bells toll a new hour, kneeling beneath a carved face that seems to gaze down into mine and noticing, to my left, corkboard, thumbtacks, slips of paper. One prayer scrawled for the teenagers in the binder. On a second prayer slip I write the names: *Jennifer and Maresa.*

The call comes as you're driving us back to the land of trucks and pines. I put it on speakerphone. The sisters no longer live together. The older girl is with people who want to adopt her. The younger girl is in what they call a "therapeutic temporary foster home." Waiting for what they call a "forever family." Us.

The six-year-old. Seven, actually; she just turned.

"That's a shame they're already split," you say. "We would gladly have taken both." They were separated, we learn, because they were fighting. "Oh, sisters," we say.

"Well, apparently the girls are calmer when apart," says the voice on the speakerphone, the voice of God, who is female (makes sense to me), with a determined uplift at the end of each sentence. We are hardly breathing, we should probably pull over. The fields outside flying past.

"Ma-REE-sa — or is it Ma-RESS-a?" says the speakerphone. "She hit her teacher with the cast on her broken arm, back in the spring. And it looks like there were a few incidents with the current foster mom ..." The voice is reading this docket for the first time, trying to find the right tone with each line.

"The girl pulled the foster mom's hair while the foster mom was driving on the freeway. Oh — eeks. So hard they almost crashed."

Later, they'll lump it all as *mild aggressions*, but I took down specifics, because that's what I do, because specifics are my faith. We were different people back when I wrote those notes, a year and a half ago. No longer in the first blush of marriage, not knowing what the final shape of our marriage would be. I hung up and felt the velocity of the family-appropriate Subaru we'd just acquired flying past the fallow fields. It was late in the year, we were heading toward winter. Our backyard garden withering.

"She *is* only the first child we've asked about," you say, and I turn back to the window.

I'm thinking not of the tomato plants I raised from seed now rotting into blackened vines, but the seedlings in plastic trays that shriveled right after sprouting.

"But don't you think they'll all be a little bit angry?" I say. "Wouldn't *you* be?"

Angry, or terrified, or just plain numb, that was the sad-dog parade of emotional states the foster services agency showed us in video after video.

"Some kids act out," the trainer said. "And some just hunker down and turn off all their feelings. A-students in school, no discipline problems, model kids. For a time."

High-functioning, I wrote, passing you a note. What I meant: *That was me*. "You're very high-functioning." What the college psychologist declared that spring day of junior year, the day I said I was afraid of myself, I'd been thinking too much about the night when I was ten and I woke up to all the blood in the hall and the glimpse of my father on the gurney. The knife taken from our own kitchen, all else undisturbed — too intimate to be random, and you know the way he was living he had something coming, people said.

"Unsolved murder," that's what they call it in TV shows and movies, and they say you're supposed to want justice, but all I ever wanted was sleep. The college psychologist pausing as though to confirm my fears of freakishness. Asking if I'd ever "gotten help."

The short answer back then: Not really. Unless I counted my mother taking me to a fluorescent-lit office the morning after all the blood. The psychiatrist handing her a prescription for Valium to mix with a spoon of peanut butter for me nightly. Which worked. Ten years of hunkering down. Until, in college, I made straight A's. And left steak knives stabbed into boxes, wondering what my roommate would say.

"High-functioning" wasn't much of a screen. Through the eyes of the man who became my first husband: "I *had* to take care of you. You were like this sweet dog that had been beaten and abused and never given a chance."

I couldn't decide whether to be grateful or offended, the first time the man who became my ex-husband told me that, back in that other life.

"Maybe a child being angry on the surface is better? So we can help the child now, not have repressed demons rise up later," I tell you.

The worker from the far-off county is coming to our house with another binder. So we can size the girl up.

So the far-off county can size us up.

"Buying pansies in October?" the nursery clerk had asked. They hang from the porch as the disclosure worker sets a manila envelope on our dining room table. We can take notes, but no photocopies, she says. You are ready with your yellow legal pad, posture straight as a schoolboy's. If I stopped to really look at you, delicate and serious as the day we decided to marry, I'd crack. But I'm distracted by the pansies, purple against grey skies.

Too desperate?

The information in the binder.

Think on it a week, the worker says.

But I can't help myself, never could. We stand a few minutes in the kitchen, afterimages of little girl swinging on monkey bars, little girl flashing jazz hands, little girl cannonballing into a pool, pictures palpable as fall sunlight breaking.

"Well, I know she said to take a week, but . . . which way are you leaning? Think we should do it?"

Three days ago you worried a child might smash your vintage records. Now you don't blink.

"Of course."

⌒

The information in the binder is hard to shake. The disconnect between the photo of a young mother nuzzling two toddlers and the facts of meth, heroin, hotels, prostitution is a black hole the imagination falls down.

"The mom looks like she was sweet," you'd said. "Like she was trying." We'd taken this as a positive. At least the little girl has known what it feels like to be loved.

Then one day there's a new photo. In a text message from the current foster mom. *She did her own hair this morning, isn't it sweet? See you in a few days!* Dimples. Chewy cheeks and an indent like someone put a finger in a pie. I rush home and flash the phone, bounce like a teenager confiding her new crush.

"She looks . . . big," you say.

If I'm honest with myself, I had the same first thought.

"Doesn't this foster mom have a six-year-old living with her, too?" you say. "Maybe we should ask about her? I just mean — let's stay aware of all our options."

I can be sanctimonious about love.

That's not how it works, I say. It has to feel fated, I say. Like when I met you.

You hold me on your lap, you hang your head. Rare moment of contrition, we've each granted the other a few. "Thank you for helping me understand."

What I don't bring up: my ex-husband. That felt fated, too, at the time.

I guess I think I know something about falling in love because I've always done it heedlessly. Not just my ex-husband. All those years, all those men. Crash and burn, crash and burn.

But now it's five years with you, Sebastian my lamb. No crash, no burn.

And when we drive back from meeting her, you're in a bigger swoon than I. You're the one who asks me to put the right music on the car stereo. The one who says, "I want to listen to something . . . hopeful."

A megamall church, that was the scene. "Dear God, don't let that red Durango with the NRA bumper sticker be her car." Little girls climbing out. Text message chiming. *You guys almost here? We parked near the front. Just look for the red Durango!*

We sit in stadium-style bleachers as the praise band tunes. "This is a little more . . . *modern* than our church," we tell the woman with feathery hair. "Auntie," the foster girls call her, because she doesn't intend to become their mother — "God didn't put adoption in my heart, but He did give me a calling to help these girls," she told us on the phone a few days ago. The ten-year-old clinging to her thigh has lived with her for two years, the six-year-old poking her for a crayon, for two months; until someone offers "permanency," that's the limbo they're in. And between you and me sits Maresa — Ma-REE-sa, as we've taken to correcting the social workers — searching for words in a puzzle. Every time she circles one we cheer like she's cracked string theory: "Good job!"

When we stand for the first song, her head barely reaches our waists. Rock concert lights flash, lyrics roll down a massive screen. "I can't read," Maresa says sadly, while the electric guitar begins to thrum, the drum set thunders in. We flash a smile at Auntie, pretend this is our kind of hallelujah. Sneak glances at the tiny creature between us, afraid of making her self-conscious. The praise band singers raising their hands, swaying with closed eyes. *If my heart is overwhelmed, and I cannot hear your voice . . .*

"*I* know this song!" the tiny creature shouts as the chords crescendo toward the chorus. Bounces. Opens her mouth wide enough to swallow the world.

You'll tell all our friends and family about that sound. The resonance! The pitch! A perfect fifth above the melody, innately harmonized. Later, we'll both call it the sound of hope.

Later. So many sounds she'll make, later. The girl can scream like a knife to the eardrum. She knows it. Looking you dead in the eye. "I'm going to scream so loud your *ears bleed.*"

Past midnight. Her voice piercing the bedroom walls and traveling through the black. Will the neighbors call 911? Should we?

"GET AWAY FROM ME! GET AWAY FROM ME! I HATE YOU! YOU DON'T LOVE ME!"

For me, this is not a new scene. I was the girl doing the screaming, back then, in college, and for too many years after. Not at my father. At all the surrogate fathers. Standing on the bed at two in the morning, threatening to throw anything within reach. Wailing like a feral animal.

"But I *do* love you," the man who became my first husband said. Again and again and again.

My life is an open book. Specifically: a memoir. Written during my first marriage and published just before I filed for divorce. About the blood in the hall and the body on the gurney

and what it took to get over it. Because sometimes, with hard
work, people do get over it. A fundamental reason we signed on
for this: I believed that whatever a kid had gone through, a kid
could get over it. With enough time. With enough understanding. I figured I would empathize.

You stare at Maresa in naked bafflement. I am not baffled.
That's me. The way I screamed at those surrogate fathers.
    "You're going to be okay," I whisper. Reaching.
    "Get AWAY!" she screams. As though my touch burns.
Clawing the air, my arms, my shoulders.
    God, Max, forgive me.

"I was baffled," my ex-husband once told me, "but I had to try
to help you, you were just a pup." Condescending, yes. He was
seven years older, after all. And I: I was twenty-three when we
met, but inside I was ten.
    Max has a scar on his shoulder. From the night I clawed him.

The sting of small fingernails. Bright liquid red in a thin line
across middle-aged skin.
    I am not baffled by this screaming girl but my comprehen-
sion is no help. She is retching, she is shaking, she is spitting up
bile. Gasping between dry heaves.
    You fetch the Band-Aids. Say to me, "Are you okay?" Say
weakly to the girl, "It's okay, you're safe." As her voice echoes past
the dead garden, down the dark streets, through the woods.

Two

AND JUST LIKE THAT, there's a new you. With a history we hardly know. A *you* we hope will become part of *us*.

You: daughter. Little and fierce. You come with scars. Broken nose, broken chin, broken arm, all acquired before age five. And mysterious marks on your thighs, lines thin as razor blades. In your pajamas, as I trace them with my finger, you say you got them in some kind of fall, but I don't see how that could be. The lines are so precise.

Right away, we add to the record of injury. "Pre-placement," they call this overnight visit, a test run before move-in.

Which was going pretty well until Daddy took you along to feed the neighbors' cats. The neighbors' gas heater left on high, the fireplace ablaze as you dashed across the room. "Daddy, come warm your hands by the fire!" you called.

And I'm not there to keep your hands safe. I'm home waiting on the back porch. I just see you running across freshly fallen snow, as the man I once knew as Sebastian but will now forever think of as "Daddy" runs after. As he shouts, "Sorry, Mommy, we've had a little accident!"

At the clinic, we're all a sobbing mess. You've been howling for two hours, you've been trying so hard to be brave, and we've been babbling, "We're sorry, so sorry, it's breaking our hearts to see you in pain, it's all our fault, we're so sorry."

The nurse practitioner wrapping up second-degree burns.

"We've just met, we're adopting her," we explain, because we must look like the most sham parents on the planet.

The nurse practitioner is wet-eyed, too. "It's beautiful," she says.

We're on alert for beauty. Searching for signs. A double rainbow on Christmas Eve Day as we drive you back to the foster home you'll soon leave. Then a bald eagle soaring as we drive back again, drive you home forever, or so we've promised, leaving Auntie and your foster sisters in the Krispy Kreme parking lot. All your belongings stuffed in two duffel bags and a blue Rubbermaid bin.

I'm the first to spot him, the black wings, white head, passing above the windshield and gliding toward the buttes. We crane our necks, gasp. "That's very rare, to see a bald eagle," Daddy says. "A good omen."

Only you never actually saw it, no matter how hard we tried to direct your eyes. You just have to believe us.

And there are some signs I never share with you, Little One. Signs I wouldn't want you to hear about until the time is right, if ever that day comes. Dark signs that hold out the hope, to me at least, of light. The week after I tacked your name to the prayer board, when you were still just a name and a picture, I drove with Daddy down to the bay again, saw him off to his classes again, climbed the hill to the cathedral for morning prayer. *And, we pray, give us such an awareness of your mercies, that with truly thankful hearts we may show forth your praise, not only with our lips but in our lives, by giving up our selves to your service* . . . Ambling the south of the nave on my way out, wanting to pause beneath the philosophers' window, pay my respects to the stained-glass Kierkegaard high above, my eye snagged on a display case at ground level. Beneath the glass: whips, chains, condoms. *Many children in the foster care system become victims of sexual slavery,* the placard read.

Directly above: life-size photos in black and white. Children. Teenagers. Not smiling, like the faces in the binder. Faces limp. And in the flesh, beneath the philosophers' window, a boy — a young man — balanced on a ladder, drilling holes to install more photographs.

This travelling exhibition is drawn from the holdings of the Foster Youth Museum, said the sign near him. The scream of the drill bit echoing, dying. The young man looked at me cautiously. "I'm glad you're here," I said. He smiled. Had *he* been a foster child? He looked healthy. Whole. Yes, I took it as a sign.

You move in on New Year's Day. Your first day at your new school will be January 3rd. The fourth school you'll have attended within two years.

On January 2nd, you stay in bed. Vomiting. For hours. Then dry heaves. We hold open plastic bags for your bile, place a thermometer shaped like a bunny in your mouth. Normal temperature. "I just don't see how it could be food poisoning," Daddy says. We all ate that meatloaf.

Once upon a time, I vomited for no reason, too. Or: too many reasons to face. Panic blazes strange fire-trails through the body.

"Help, Mommy," you say.

I'm not sure how I feel about that word. I didn't want you to *have* to use it. I wanted you to call me whatever felt right. I thought what you called me could evolve. But the third time we met, the foster mom with the red Durango crouched near your ear and said, not sotto voce enough, "Go hug your new mommy." And a bit later, when you said, "Bye, Mommy," she gasped in blessing.

Auntie gasped a lot that day, that day that was like a marriage proposal. An old pro in the system, she had served as "the bridge" for dozens of girls, and we were dependent on her coaching. The day before, Daddy and I had spent an hour in the toy store, debating between the brown bunny and the black bunny, stroking one and then the other, seeking ultimate soft. "Transitional object," the social workers called it. Something you could carry back and forth between your old life and your new. A stuffed polyester symbol of us. Which you were supposed to cling to while we were still strangers.

"Mr. Fluffy Stuffy Puff Ball!" you christened him over chicken tenders at Denny's. Then rubbed him against your dimpled face as though prepped by the social workers' script.

Back at Auntie's house that day, we knelt on the carpet. Showed you photos of your new bedroom, staged with model horses and vintage teddy bears. There was no popping the question per se. You don't ask a child that young, the social workers advised. You just tell her. And say that whatever she feels is okay. Daddy had designated me for the job. I had practiced.

"The tone, the body language was just perfect!" Auntie said later.

You, Little One: speechless.

The sheets I bought for your mattress have pictures of bunnies dressed in ski clothes. You hold Fluffy Stuffy Puff Ball. We read silly kid-poems about boogers and boa constrictors. We turn on night-lights.

Back at Auntie's, after we'd returned you from a "preplacement visit," you'd taught me how to kiss. Leaning over the rail of the bunk bed in the dark. "Mommy, hold your hands up like this." Making a heart with your fingers and thumb. Our lips touching in the middle of the heart-hand.

I was honored. I was disturbed. The social workers had shown me a picture of you with your birth mom, her hands held like a heart as your lips touched.

Now you roll out a dozen new kisses. It goes on for half an hour, the bedtime kissing, all three of us speaking too brightly. Butterfly kiss! Eskimo kiss! Bunny ears kiss! Shooting star kiss! More kisses, Daddy! More kisses, Mommy!

"We love you!" we say.

"I love you more!"

"That can't be true! Because we love you *soooooooo* much!" We've talked about this, Daddy and I. We want to walk you away from this idea of love as a contest, logic that can come to no good.

You look at us with the bitter disillusionment of a girl whose boyfriend was too cheap to buy Valentine's roses. "You're supposed to say I love you more plus infinity."

One night you put your thumbs and forefingers together and then you fan the rest of your fingers as you bring your lips between your hands. "Bald eagle kiss!" you announce. And as Daddy and I draw back in astonishment, you make a shape with your hands that no one would guess was a bird. "See, these are the wings, and in the middle, this is the bald head."
    "Oh, we see it!" we say. A dozen bald eagle kisses.
    "That was a good omen," Daddy confirms.

Another new kiss. No warning. My lips are pressed to yours, and then I feel your wet tongue probing, and I spring backward.
    "I don't like that kiss," I say. Reminding myself not to scowl. Speaking with the fake brightness. As you giggle.
    You do it again the next night. You say, "Mommy, take a shower with me."
    You twirl around the living room with no panties on, stop in front of where I sit on the sofa, bend over and spread your little naked crotch inches from my face.

There's a new social worker from the far-off county. He's Chinese American, all Californian: flip-flops in February, slouchy hoodies, "yeahs" and "heys." "Do you think he surfs?" I joke with Daddy. I like him.
    He drives up and down the state visiting the kids on his caseload. Apparently he met you the day you were taken from your birth mom, though it's unclear whether you remember. He'll visit once a month until we finalize. Which, since your mother's parental rights are all but officially terminated, we ex-

pect will happen as soon as the minimum six months of foster placement pass.

He slouches in his hoodie as you dash to your bedroom to don your too-tight old dance costumes and grab your pink plastic microphone. He speaks low as you ready yourself, off-stage, for the elaborate, manic performance you rally for all our visitors.

"So the crotch stuff, yeah . . . in cases like this, you just can't know everything that happened. But uh, so I went to a conference on sexual abuse last week. And the presenter was saying . . . conservative estimate for foster kids and sexual abuse? Probably sixty percent."

You're equal opportunity with your daytime tauntings, Little One: You'll get on all fours and wave your rectum at me and Daddy both. Giggle and beg us to get your booty. But bedtime is different. You'll let me lie down in your bed to help you fall asleep, but Daddy? No. You don't slip Daddy the tongue. And already you've said to me twice: "Mommy, why do I feel weird snuggling Daddy? Is it because he's a boy?"

You don't tell us about your mom's boyfriends, don't talk about the nights in the hotels. You tell us about the afternoon with the frying pan, how your grandmother dragged your mom into the back room and slammed the door and then you heard the whack. How your mom came out covered in blood. We hear about other kitchen implements. "One time, my birth mom? She took a spatula, and she was so angry, and she pulled down my pants and she hit me, over and over. *Hard.*" You say this apropos of nothing one night, between bites of macaroni while Daddy is staying overnight in San Francisco to teach his

art classes. I'm fumbling for a script: Do I press you for more?
The only lines I feel sure of: I'm so sorry, sweetie; that shouldn't
have happened.

"Oh. It was nothing." Artificial cheese glaring orange on your
plate.

We hear again and again about the spatula. And about the
magic forest.

We made a house with branches because we had nowhere to stay.
It was raining but the leaves covered us. We drank raindrops out
of the flowers. The flowers were our cups. We had no money for
food but the trees had tiny purple apples and we ate them and
they were sweet. I was happy because we had raindrops to drink
from the flowers. I slept with my mom and my sister in the magic
forest.

At midnight, this is what you tell me to write, because you
can't go back to sleep. We are sitting on the floor in a circle
of lamplight. Your therapist taught me about "life books," how
I could offer to write down your memories, a directive I was
happy to run with, as someone who credits writing for ending
those years of stabbing knives into boxes. A life book will help
you "externalize," the therapist said. I should go ahead and help
you name your emotions if you're not able. And so I lift the
purple-inked pen from the construction paper.

"Honey, was it cold in the house made of branches? It sounds
kind of scary to have no money for food."

"Oh no, it wasn't scary. We were happy. There were fairies!"

We're driving home from gymnastics when I spot highway pa-
trol in the rearview mirror. Daddy's away for work again and
night is thickening between the pines.

When the cop car passes you say, "Why did the policeman push my mom on the ground?"

I catch your eye in the mirror, but my gaze contains more question than reply.

"She was crying and they pushed her on the ground! Policemen are mean!"

Over that night's macaroni, I ask if you know what drugs are.

"Like the stuff a doctor gives you when you're sick and then you feel better?"

Yes, I say, and change the subject to your cartwheels.

Daddy returns when you're asleep and tells me the words to type into the search box. "I couldn't help myself," he says.

I've drawn my hand to my mouth. Nausea reflex. The room darkens, though the screen is too bright. The unmistakable fluorescent pallor of a mug shot. Her face is blue-green-grey, purple below the eyes, a stripe of electric red hair above. This is not the same mother I saw in the disclosure photos the day I worried about the pansies. This woman is the walking dead.

A second face. His head is bald. Tattoo around his neck. And on his scalp, more markings — devil's horns.

A gun was involved. The man with the devil horns used it. Assault. Robbery.

And then the last line of the newspaper report: *Two children of the female accomplice, ages four and six, were taken by Child Welfare Services at the time of arrest.*

The room dimming as though a dark spell has been cast, and we're frozen, trying to identify an antidote. "I don't think we should show this to anyone," Daddy says. "Okay? We'll just keep what we've seen between us."

You tend to bring up your birth mom when Daddy's not around. Which is every Tuesday through Thursday, when he takes the train down to the Bay Area and stays two nights, to teach his art classes.

I've expanded my kid food repertoire to include pizza poppers. "Oh! I think I remember what my birth mom looked like," you say as you watch the red sauce ooze. "Her hair was red. Like, a stripe."

"Really?" I say, fake bright. "You mean, like a streak she dyed?"

"Oh, no." You're nodding stridently. "Her hair was naturally red. She *never* dyed it."

We say that you can always love your birth mom. That you don't have to choose. That the way love works, you can always have more of it.

I had two moms, I explain, my birth mom (your new grandma) and my dad's second wife, the one he left right before he died, the one who still sends me birthday cards. I love them both and that's okay. "In fact, if you want," I tell you, "we can write a letter to your birth mom."

Your eyes wide. "And then we could go visit?"

So I don't go back to the idea of letter writing for a while. Until one night when I insist that we clean your room, that night when just asking you to put the Play-Doh back in the canisters starts you screaming, and then you run to the living room and carry on there.

Daddy is frying chicken in the kitchen, the grease hissing

as you wail. We're both on the living room floor, you writhing as though on fire, and then you're shouting, "MOMMY! MY MOMMY! I MISS MY MOMMY!"

"I'm so sorry," I say. "I'm so sorry you can't see her." Grab pen and paper. "Let's write to her," I say. And you sit up, suddenly focused, eyes wet and glaring. "There's a string between our hearts. Write that. Write: Dear Mommy, there's a string between our hearts no matter how far away we go. Write: Dear Mommy, I love you. Absolutely."

Where did you learn that word? Daddy and I will marvel over that later. Absolutely: the perfect word for the truth of the matter.

"Absolutely," you repeat.

I meet alone with your therapist and ask for a script. She was the first therapist offered by the county, and I feel lucky that I like her. She's about my age, on or just past the brink of forty, and though she's blonde, she looks like me, in a way — we could fill the same stock character role in a movie. She dresses like me, too, or at least the way I used to dress until my last day childless: tailored jeans, dangly earrings. She even moved from the Bay Area to the foothills about the same time I did, so she could take this job working with foster kids. She has a cyst-like bump on her left cheek, too pale for a mole. I once saw her tell you it's her "bimple."

She operates under the auspices of the foster services agency that matched us with you and has an office in their cinderblock building. The discreet kneeling movement she makes to click on the whirring white-noise machine before closing the door impresses me.

"We recommend that your explanations stay age-appropriate," she says. "You can just say: Your birth mother is safe but she can't take care of children right now. She's glad that you're safe."

The next night on the futon, I follow this word-for-word, one arm around your shoulder.

"But why can't we visit her?"

I'm alone in the car in the gymnastics parking lot when the surfer dude social worker from the far-off county calls. I'm not quite sure what to explain about the birth mom, I tell him. Do you tell a seven-year-old that her mom is in jail?

"Yeah, well, actually, right now her mom's back out," surfer dude says as though to amuse. "You know, actually, she came into our office last week asking about the girls, but I wasn't there. She didn't leave a message."

Fuck is the word that comes to mind.

"I mean, I guess we didn't talk about this yet, but you know, down the line . . . how do you guys feel about visits?"

"She scares me," I say.

A laugh. "Yeah, she does have a certain persona."

Blue hair. Black hoodie. Black eyeliner. Blue glitter eye shadow.

There she is wearing headphones. There she is wearing purple lipstick. There she is holding your sister. There she is kissing you.

This is what I found on Facebook.

The photos were posted last year, but in them you must be four, five. She hasn't seen you since. Just posted old pictures and feelings. *A mother loves her children more than her own life. Reshare if you agree.*

⌒

And in the next post, there she is alone. Flipping off the camera. An orange hotel room bedspread behind her. A caption.

*Fuck all you all hatin ass muthafuckas cuz I woke up White
and Winning.*

Shock is an insufficient word. Bafflement. You and your sister, Little One: You're brown. The only thing we know about
your birth dad is that his name is Chavez. You said to us once,
"You're white and I'm black." We tried to explain about African
Americans. We taught you the word "Latina."

If I'm honest with myself, part of me is relieved to see the
racist post.

Your mother was the daughter of meth addicts. The social
workers tell us she was hooked by thirteen. Got her first hit
from her parents. Started shooting it at seventeen. She was a
victim before she was a gang member. I have to remind myself.
She did try to get clean, when she first lost you. I think she did
try. But the racist post settles the matter: She's too sick to be
your mother.

"People can see who's been looking at their profiles!" Daddy
whispers while you sleep.

I say I won't do it again. But then I open an account under
an alias for the purpose.

*Jennifer Ann and Maresa Michelle where ever you are just know
I am always with you in your heart and I love you more than anything in this whole wide world and some day when fate brings us
back together where we belong know that nothing will ever tear us
apart again.*

ᕲ

There are photos of a new tattoo across her shoulder blades, posts about hitting high scores on iPhone games involving aliens. A location check-in pegged to a Super 8. But no more posts about those words too disturbing for me to type.

"Your birth mom is happy you're safe and with a loving family." The therapist told me to repeat that.

HAPPY MOTHERS DAY to you bitches blessed To be mothers and to the ones lucky enough to keep you're children and even also happy fuckin mothers day to us who have had our beautiful children stollen by the goverment (tho Im sure that's the last fuckin thing you want someone to say bc every time some bitch says that to me I ball my fuckin eyes out) SHAME on the cops for praying on our weakness They rip our kids away bc we dont have the money to fight back Take from the God damn poor and give to the fuck In rich its just a little fuckin much FUCK THEM ALL except mothers I love you and the people who steel our children go fuckin rot

Daddy and I never used to pray over meals, but you learned to do that at Auntie's, so now every night, to make you comfortable, we bring our hands together and bow and you lead. *Dear Heavenly Father, thank you for the things you have gaven us, like the birds and the flowers so sweet, and the animals, and the sky. And thank you for the world, because I really like it.*

Daddy says, "We can also pray for your birth mother."

Aloud: "We hope Maresa's birth mom is healthy and safe, and we want her to know Maresa loves her forever."

Silently: I'm stumped.

⌒

Inconclusive thought experiment: If, by miracle, your birth mother got her life together and left the gang and truly kicked the meth and the heroin — if she wanted you back, and you wanted to be reunited with her — would I support that? Would I be happy for you two?

The bald eagle kiss is my favorite. I want it every night. You wait for me to ask. Then you hold up your hands and spread your fingers and look left and right to check the shape before bringing it to your mouth. Saying, "Wait, *wait.*" Touching index fingers to lips. "See the *bald* head in the middle?"

"I do," I say. "I love you!"

"I love you more!"

"I love you more plus infinity!"

"I love you more plus infinity *plus* infinity!"

Our little church here in the foothills is hardly a cathedral; still, you're dazzled. "There are *candles*," you say. And a choir, which I haven't sung with since you moved in. Too dicey, I thought, to miss your bedtime for rehearsal. "You'll have to miss a bedtime at *some* point," Daddy says.

We follow the therapist's coaching, prep you for days. Explain that I'll be back while you sleep; I'll be the first thing you see in the morning. That Daddy will keep you safe. But that night, after dinner, you throw yourself on my leg. I hug you; you hug me tighter. I wrench myself away; you wail, "NOOOOOO!"

"It's okay, just go," Daddy says. "You deserve this, hurry!"

I drive too fast on the gravel beneath the chestnut trees, toward the darkness between the pines, not knowing if I'm more afraid of leaving or staying. In the rearview mirror I see Daddy

chasing after you, all the way to the end of the driveway, down
the street.

My heart pounds like a criminal's.

And that voice of yours, how it carries. "Mommy, Mommy, I
NEEEEEED Mommy!"

The day we told you we would be your forever family, right before we popped the question, we took you to JCPenney. Auntie
said it was your turn among the girls to pick out new clothes,
so Daddy and I tagged along, Daddy pink-faced and fidgety in
the little girls' panties department. You said you needed to pee
and I took you to the bathroom. You strained and flushed and
zipped and I lifted you to the sink to wash your hands and you
said, "I like this. It's like you're my mom." And in that badly lit
bathroom I felt aglow.

But when we were looking through the racks again you said
you wanted gloves. "I met a woman at my school who said she
lives in the snow? And I really hope I go live with her."

Suddenly the windowless department store felt dark as a
cave.

That day, back at Auntie's, you strapped on roller skates. Up
and down the concrete patio, up and down as Daddy cheered.
And then — boom. On your bottom. Face of shock. You held
up something gold and shiny, you said, "I hate it when I fall
on these." Then your face melted from shock to pain, but you
didn't run to me, of course you didn't, we'd spent all of six hours
together. I stepped aside, helped you run to Auntie. And as you
cried, I knew beyond doubt what I wanted, two things: That
you'd never again have to slip on a bullet casing. And that you'd
run to me.

"God, when she held up that bullet casing," Daddy said after our next visit to Auntie's, the last pre-placement visit before you came to stay overnight, then came *home*. We were in the restaurant we liked, with the deck above the creek, for one of the last times. "No more going out for a glass of wine just because we feel like it," Daddy said. We'd been at the roller rink with you half the day, our ears still ringing with the screams of hyperstimulated children. We were drinking more wine than usual.

"Why are we doing this, exactly?" Daddy said.

I thought of one of my favorite writers, the line in her story about having a child more because she was afraid of *not* having a child than because she truly wanted one. I thought of her story "Selfish." In it, the mother is just a little bit selfish. In it, the child's life is a disaster, and this is due to the mother's selfishness. I thought of Daddy's favorite painter, Philip Guston. How Guston resented his daughter for interrupting his painting, and she knew it, and it crushed her. I thought that if Daddy were more of an asshole, maybe he'd have more of an art career.

We listened to the creek and thought our silent thoughts and ordered another glass. Clinked. "To going all in," Daddy finally said.

But now you're racing after me in the rearview mirror, and you're getting smaller in the distance, and I'm pressing harder on the gas.

Is it me you're running after? Your birth mother? Any mother?

Does it even matter which?

Three

So THERE'S ME (Mommy) and there's you (Daddy) and there's you (Little One). And then there's *them*.

A lot of them.

I was confident I wouldn't mind *them*. I have no secrets; after all, I wrote a memoir. I'm the definition of indiscreet. Daddy's the private one. He turns sullen when I blab that he has a heart defect. I forget to tap-dance around telling people what to me is daily reality. To him, eyes flaring: "Honey! That's private."

Atrial septal defect, to be exact. Patched together in a surgery a year before I met him. Prognosis: as good as anyone could hope. Still, he feared it would be a mark against him in the home study.

Symptoms: dizziness, fatigue, shortness of breath.

He lied a bit. For the home study. Said the symptoms were never so bad that he had to miss a day of work.

Me, I presumed I had nothing to hide. *I made it out the other side! Murdered father, unsolved case, asshole stepfather. Faced it all!* Congenital shamelessness of the memoirist.

The interviewers, back when the memoir came out, oohed and aahed. They used descriptors in their articles that made me uncomfortable: "brave" and "inspiring."

The agency social worker who interviewed us for the home study was another story. She stopped taking notes, cocked her small, grey-crowned head, and regarded me in the manner of a doctor breaking news to a sick patient. "Huh. So. How do you handle anger?"

When problems arise, a parent who doesn't understand [her] own trauma may feel like [her] child is deliberately trying to manipulate [her].

This sentence appears in *Wounded Children, Healing Homes*, a book the grey-crowned social worker has twice advised me to read. A book I cannot bring myself to finish.

Another book the worker tells me is "highly regarded among the child welfare community": *Beyond Consequences, Logic, and Control.*

The traumatized child becomes the associational connection to the parent's unresolved trauma and loss issues, state the coauthors, *shifting the parent into a deep fear state.*

"And here I thought my experiences would be a *bonus*," I said to Daddy at bedtime.

"They're programmed to see lifelong pathology," he said. "Nothing outside that computes."

This was months before we met you, and we were up late

fretting because the grey-crowned social worker who was writ-ing our home study had called for a fourth interview. The home study she would write was the dossier workers from all the far-off counties would use to choose potential matches. In other words: our ticket to meeting you.

"So," the grey-crowned social worker asked again the next day, sitting in our living room, "how do you handle anger?"

I see, or think I see, the necessity of repeating the question. When it comes to anger management, Little One, not many grownups in your life seem to have practiced it. Not just your birth mom and her boyfriends, but also your former foster par-ents. That was abstract to me and Daddy until your first pre-placement visit. Until Daddy saw you holding the cat's paws to the heating vent and shouted, "Don't do that!" And you ran and hid, trembling, in your closet.

"I wasn't shouting because I was angry," Daddy said, and you paused from whimpering. "I was just worried about the cat."

Almost a whisper: "Is this the kind of family that shouts a lot?"

No, we promised you. No, we pledged to ourselves. We are not going to shout in this family. No.

"We" is often ambiguous. Turns out "we are not going to shout" meant *you* would shout, but *we* would never, ever, under threat of eternal shame and self-recrimination, shout back.

Proposal for a new bumper sticker, to stick alongside the ones advertising that your child made honor roll: THESE PARENTS DO NOT SHOUT AT THEIR DAUGHTER.

I'd say for your first month with us we're not angry. Just irritated. But you seem bent on getting us pissed.

We ask you not to slide down the dirt pile in the backyard until you're in play clothes; you throw yourself upon it.

We play hide-and-seek with you and declare anything outside the fence is off limits; you giggle behind a tree across the street while we search frantically.

We say, "Now wait for us to cross the street or else we'll need to hold hands!"; you dash right out in front of traffic.

"We don't *want* to punish you," we say softly.

"You have to be firm!" you respond. "Auntie was firm!"

What do you mean by "firm"?

Someone was always getting in trouble at Auntie's, punishments continually meted. Writing sentences: *I will not hit my foster sister.* Losing dessert, or dinner. Getting sent to bed early over infractions like taking one too many chicken nuggets, or saying "hell" or "God," or (this rule especially pained us) letting your belly button show when your shirt flipped up on the monkey bars. "Do you really want that many rules still?" we ask. "Too complicated!" we tease.

But maybe what you mean by "firm" is that actually you *want* us to shout. "Kids who are used to it often crave that kind of intensity," the grey-crowned social worker has warned us.

The second time Daddy catches you holding the cat's paws up to the heater, he says, "Now, Maresa," in a voice I would call calm. Maybe unnervingly so.

At which your face spasms like water about to boil. "Go ahead! *Scream* at me! I *knew* you'd be just like Joe!"

Joe, the foster dad at the second home you ended up in, the home you lived in for a year with your sister.

Daddy is nothing like Joe. I hope you sense this. "You're weird, but you're kinda awesome," you said on Auntie's carpet, moments before we announced we'd be your parents. And when you said that to Daddy my heart sang. By "weird" you might have meant his thinness and his quietness, or the fact that a fifty-something man was sitting with you on the floor saying he liked your drawing. But I suppose he's weird in other ways, too, compared to men you've known. He wears thrift store V-neck sweaters and raises orchids and spends more time tending the bird feeder than pumping iron. Truth be told, I've shouted at Daddy a time or two. He has never shouted back.

Which isn't to say he can't be intimidating. Hard to read. *Sebastian is blonde and thin and of medium height and speaks with flat affect,* the grey-crowned social worker wrote in the home study, *though he will brighten up when you engage him on certain subjects.* A line that made me laugh, remembering those stilted early dates.

Mainly though, Little One, you back off on Daddy. Save the worst of the morning screaming for when Daddy is out of town. The descriptor "tantrum" does not suffice to convey the aural reality of these episodes to anyone I confide in. So one morning when Daddy's in San Francisco and I'm trying to get you to put your shoes on, I press the red Record button on the phone.

"I need you to take deep breaths and stop yelling, Maresa. My heart is racing. *Here,* feel. Okay? Let's take deep breaths."

"I'M NOT YELLING! YOU'RE THE ONE YELLING! STOP YELLING!"

"But I'm not yelling, Maresa. I'm not yelling."

When I play it back hours later, the voices don't sound the way I expect. The child is screeching, yes. The woman I hear isn't yelling, that's true. But the calm in her voice is almost worse somehow — eerie, like a captor's.

I send the sound file to Daddy. Then to surfer dude. But within minutes, I wish I hadn't. What am I doing here, snitching? What do I expect the worker to do, give you a time-out?

Another thought that comes to mind as I listen to the play-back: *Honey! That's private.*

He's had a few weak spells since you moved in, afternoons when he lay down, shaking. Once, he even skipped driving down to teach his classes.

"I won't get to make my art now," he says one night as we lie in bed. "I'll have to spend all my time taking care of Maresa and you, and teaching, and trying to make enough money."

"We'll make the time," I say. I've been nagging him to turn the garage into a studio. "You should work on those watercolors again. And those little etchings you were doing, those were so weird and beautiful." My vision, when we married: I would write and he would paint, and we'd never give either up.

"Maresa's more important," he says. And then the old refrain, the one I suspect he'd say even if he were healthy and alone: "No one wants my art anyway."

⌒

"I want it," I say, and he kisses me the way he used to back when we were alone in his apartment for the first time. All the paintings he'd never sold covering every inch of wall and rolled up beneath the bed.

There are more than a dozen reasons I married Daddy, but here's #3: his honesty in those last moments before sleep.

"You can't worry about the workers watching you," he says into the dark. The snow that used to fall so reliably upon the pines is, these days, an anomaly. Rain is pattering the garden beds, small relief in this long drought. In the morning there will be frost.

"You're right," I say. Feel for the pulse in his wrist. "Do you think . . ." Fall silent. "Did we make the right choice?"

His pulse, for many beats, is the only response. Then: "If we can keep everyone safe and help this little girl, yes."

I agree, intellectually, but the answer seems abstract. Only the questions feel real. That winter afternoon, when Daddy's teaching class, you come home with extra weight in your backpack, and I remember the yellow notice that went home about the used-book fair, flip through your selection. Drawings of smiling, long-eyelashed insects, a picture of what looks to be some kind of big green bug cradling a little spider. Inside, my eye catches on a line of text. Out of all those boxes of free books, you chose one that says, *For finding your mother, there's one certain test.*

"Sit down next to me here and let's read this," I say when I can breathe again. I want to know, as soon as possible, how it ends.

Four

You and you and I and *them*. You don't get a choice about all
the *thems*. Whereas, technically, Daddy and I have some choice.
Technically.

*Did you know that the agency also offers a Family Support Special-
ist who partners with your therapist?*
    Why no, I didn't!
    Would you like to avail yourselves of this?
    Why yes, of course!
    *Did you know the Family Support Specialist can also do home
visits?*
    Ah, I had no idea!
    Do you think that might help?
    Sure! Let's try it!

The Family Support Specialist is like Skipper to your therapist's blonde Barbie. Short, brunette. Wears heels and belted
dresses. Not so cheery, though. She slumps back in her chair after handing me a "safety workbook" featuring Timmy the Tur-

tle. "Kids and animals," she says in the tone of a weary diner waitress.

"See, the key to positive parenting is *constant* incentivizing," she adds, handing over the laminated points chart like a salesman angling to make quota.

Did you know that the Family Support Specialist can also visit the school to do a classroom observation?
    Why, no!
    Would you like that?
    Well, sure!

Already the books are blurring into one another. *Traditional parenting techniques assume an intact child-parent attachment. Where no such attachment yet exists, punishments that depend on the child's motivation to reconnect to the parents, such as time-outs, simply will not work.*

"Do they ever say what *does* work?" Daddy asks, reading the stacks of papers the Family Support Specialist sent home. "God, we're greenhorns. We're gonna need all the help we can get."

It was Daddy who came up with the system of marking the calendar next to the back door with checks. Each time you shout at us or refuse to do what's asked, you'll get a check. No checks for three days in a row, you get a dollar. One or two checks in a day, no consequences. Three checks, you'll lose dessert. In executing this system, we strive to imitate your Auntie's sweet but firm tone. "Okay, now I've asked you three times to come with me to the bathroom and brush your teeth. If I have to ask you *again*, sweetie, it's going to be a check."

At which you run to the back door, throw your body in front of the calendar like you're stopping a speeding train, and claw at the arm I'm using to make the mark. "NO CHECK! NO CHECK! NO CHECK!"

"The checks seem to be triggering her," the blonde therapist with the bimple says.

The new laminated chart on the refrigerator is pink, with five categories: *Get dressed, Eat breakfast respectfully, Brush hair, Brush teeth, Make bed.* Important to focus on just one daily routine at a time, the Family Support Specialist says.

"Did she get three points for brushing teeth today, or would you say that's more like two?"

"Definitely two," Daddy says.

"What about breakfast?"

"Well, after the screaming . . ."

"But she did come back out of the closet and eat a few bites. Let's say that's one and a half?"

School is complicated, too. Choice is supposed to help you feel empowered, but it seems to leave you exasperated. The other day, the teacher said you could do the worksheet with the other children, *or* you could read in the corner, *or* you could practice with the math wheel, but the scissors had to be put away. You screamed and bolted out the door. He had to rush across the four-square courts for you, carry you back. He calls after school to tell me, his voice friendly and unalarmed. He's a slight man with a dignified nose who wears corduroy slacks. He's been teaching for thirty-five years. He has a piano in his classroom, an Oriental rug spread beneath the wingback chair he sits in for story time, and plays classical CDs after roll call. He seems, to me and Daddy, the embodiment of civilized existence.

"We'll get through this," he says. "You know, parents are welcome in the classroom *anytime*."

"Boy-teachers are mean," you say.

I've gone back to teaching adult ed online, a stack of unread stories on my desk. No plan for finishing them beyond praying you actually fall asleep at nine. But Daddy's down in San Francisco for his art classes and someone has to take a ground report.

The moment I leave my desk and walk over to your school, the cramps start.

Menstruation is different in one's forties. My womb seems to be taking some kind of twisted revenge for all the conception-free pleasure I had in my twenties and thirties. I sit in a first-grader-sized chair at the back of your classroom, trying to double over as if casually slouching, rather than enduring a knife to the uterus. A floppy-haired boy holds up a family photo. "So this is my *mom*, and my *dad*, and my little brother. Um, my sister was supposed to be in it too, but she dyed her hair green?"

You are sitting on the carpet with the group, Little One, poking the girl next to you with a Crayola and then hissing like a cat. Oh, Little One. I look down to hide the gargoyle-like contortion my uterus is forcing on my face. But who would fail to smile when the boy concludes, with a professorial nod and the picture upside down, "Any questions?"

The mothers who wait with their children every morning between the first bell and the teacher's greeting at the door — one
father, too, bless him — they're all so calm and sweetly smiling
and competent. "I can't believe how big they've gotten," the father says to me by way of introduction, and I try to think of a
way to affirm our shared parental affection without burdening
him with backstory, and I fail.

I sign the parent volunteer spreadsheet for the Valentine's party
the day it goes out. Bring double the icing I'd promised, and
throw in conversation hearts for good measure. Stand dazed as
kids squeal and scream and flick Red Hots. The sign-up sheet
said a few moms were needed for supervision. So why is there
one mom for every kid?

"Isn't it too precious?" one says, before averting her gaze
from my immobile face.

Eight-thirty to 2:45: That's when you're in school, and that's
when I can teach and write.

That is, except when I'm meeting the Family Support Specialist on the blacktop for a recess observation, or going to the
school an hour early to help the PTA president make signs for
the Casino Night fundraiser, or spending half an hour on hold
with County Behavioral Health.

What I told Daddy, back when we were still in the home
study phase: "I think if I can just get four hours a day alone, I
can do this."

What I tell Daddy now: "I think if I can just get *two* hours a
day alone, I can do this."

Raymond Carver on writing with children: *There were good times back there, of course; certain grown-up pleasures and satisfactions that only parents have access to. But I'd take poison before I'd go through that time again.*

"Are you Maresa's mom?" the other mothers ask with pointed kindness. I consider the fact that I have known you all of six weeks and I am at a loss.

But I'm on a mission to get you a playdate. We choose the most with-it girl in your class, the one whose straw-blonde hair is always freshly cut. I write out an invitation for you to give her, instructing the girl to have her mother call me. Naturally it turns out her mother is the PTA president, knows every other mother at the school, and is overbooked with playdates. But because you are a new kid, she is kind.

She brings little Cassie over with her younger brother after school. You are ecstatic. You decide to serve tea, and I get down the gilt-rimmed china that thrills you, but the experience is less Buckingham Palace than Hell's Kitchen, because you want to carry the kettle and you want to pour the hot water and you want everyone to use exactly four sugar cubes, and when you reach over Cassie to stir her tea, the cups spill and the tea runs everywhere.

Sweet Little One, with your tiny teaspoons and your feet that don't quite touch the floor. You sit at the table with your open-mouthed face of embarrassment. Cassie helping you pile on paper towels, her mother rising. "Ah, sorry, we've got Wes's basketball league practice, so . . . we've really got to go!" Tight smile. "Oh, it's craziness with kids, isn't it?" she offers. "Always craziness!"

And you slipping into your baby-regressive voice. "You'll come back?" you're calling out. "Come back tomorrow!"

"Oh, we'll do it again!" Cassie's mom calls. "We'll do it soon!"

"How come Cassie doesn't talk to me at school now?" you'll ask me next week.

I see the moms at the grocery store. I see them at yoga class. I see them at the café where I read my students' stories and try to write. I see them as we leave for the walk to school every morning. "Oh, that's your house, the little yellow one on the corner!" the moms say. Eight-five-two Jordan Street, yes, that's us.

I used to get a chuckle out of the way our town paper publishes a daily police blotter. *A caller from the 1500 block of Brunswick Avenue reported that his dog has x-ray vision. A caller from the 900 block of Sutton Way reported that her daughter's boyfriend was trying to run her over.*

Now I read the addresses with a shudder.

Sometimes, Little One, I want everyone to see us. Like in church, when you sing the hymns. Surprisingly game about your new house of worship having a sanctum instead of an auditorium, an organist instead of a rock band, though you do say you miss the way, at your old church, the Sunday school teachers gave you fake money for each Bible verse you memorized.

When it's time to lift our voices, you don't settle for the melody; you go for the descant. Startling the whole congregation with your ear for the high notes. "Opera voice," you call this. "It's true," we tell everyone at coffee hour. "She's destined for the Met!"

Other times, I'd rather we didn't become the show. When you start sucking my thumb as I carry you up the aisle for communion. When you throw crayons and screech like a wet cat during the confession. When I'm singing a small solo for the offering and you rush up the aisle in a blaze of agitation, try to cover my mouth with your hand, shouting, "Stop it, Mommy, stop it!"

"And are you having fun being a mommy?" the littlest old church lady asks.

Long after she's left me standing in the parish hall with a scoop of spinach dip, I consider why it was so hard to respond. Was it the phrasing of her question that disturbed? Maybe that's the problem. This isn't supposed to be about *me*.

Of course there's a simpler explanation for my silence: The honest answer was "no."

Fun: *enjoyment, amusement, or lighthearted pleasure.*

I don't know if she looks like she's having fun, exactly, the crooked-toothed teenager who smiles at me from a gilt frame next to my desk, but she radiates a kind of pleasure. Holding up a pudge-faced baby for the drugstore photo booth, nuzzling the baby's cheek in one frame, grinning googly-eyed in the next. I discovered this photo in the garage back when Daddy and I were starting the home study phase. I stared at it dumbfounded. My mother, your future grandmother, just after my father left her to pursue his string of one-night stands. Before the sociopath second husband she would divorce when I was thirteen. "Seems like she was a really good mom who just picked some

bad men" — so said more than a few readers of my memoir. She
never smoked pot, never shouted, either. Just a plain girl from a
dead valley town. Finally married a nice guy, husband #3, after
her kids were grown.

Twice, the childless grey-crowned social worker asked if
Daddy and I really wanted to raise a kid. Both times, I thought
on these photos of my mother. Wanting to be her. Wanting
someone else to be me.

"Have some fun shopping!" my mother exhorted the week
before you moved in. So I clicked through kids' clothes until my brain buzzed like a fluorescent-lit mall. *Is life really for
this?*

Daddy gives me a Saturday off to drive down to San Francisco,
have an afternoon of hiking with my childless-and-happy-
about-it best friend. The friend I love because she'll ask point-
blank: "Okay, just between us — any regrets?"

I say there are times when you're dictating how many rai-
sins should go in the snack box, or correcting me on whether
one can exchange Chuck E. Cheese tickets for ChapStick at
CVS, and even though everything you're saying is adorable,
I'm thinking, SHUT UP SHUT UP SHUT UP SHUT UP
PLEASE JUST FOR A MOMENT SHUT UP.

"You know they wrote a book about that for parents," she
says. "Except it's about bedtime and it's called *Go the Fuck to
Sleep*, so I'd say you're doing well."

I leave for that visit on Friday, after bringing you home from
school and getting you settled. The sun is still shining. I drive to

my friend's house thinking, I'M FREE, I'M FREE, I'M FREE,
I'M FREE. By the time I get there, though, the streets are dark
and there's a message on my cell phone. "Hi, Mommy," Daddy's
voice says. "Maresa wants to talk to you." And then, a voice so
small and desperate I will never delete it: "Mommy? When are
you coming home? Mommy? I want you to come home. Okay?
Mommy? I love you."

I play it eight times. *Life is for this.*

I watch you sleep at midnight, return to my bedroom to find
Daddy readying his drawing lesson.

"You know what's crazy?" I say. "Even though it's only been a
few months, I do love her."

Daddy looks grimly over his lesson plan. Any fidelity to
his syllabi this semester is, at this point, a joke. He spent yes-
terday trying to keep you from flinging yourself off the swing
at peak height, ducking your screams of "You meanie! You
meanie!" as he drove you home from the park. The stress must
be the reason his face seems stony; it's easy to misread his re-
actions.

"Do *you* love her?"

He's taking off his glasses but he's not meeting my eyes.

"I'm struggling with some aspects of her personality, I guess.
She's loud, you know? Forceful. And . . . she doesn't really like
to read."

What the *Wounded Children, Healing Homes* book said: *The
parents must adapt rapidly, do all the initial adapting, and commit to a child they don't yet love, and may not even like, for awhile.*

⌒

"You've had a rough couple days with her," I say. "She's opening up to me right now maybe more than you. That'll shift."

"Maybe."

"I'm glad we can both be honest about our feelings," I say. "That's the important thing."

Then: Neither of us sleeps.

The next day at lunch I get a call. I almost don't take it because I'm busy that day, posting responses to student work on the screen space that's marketed as a "classroom," preparing to introduce a visiting writer friend at the little local bookstore.

It's the Family Support Specialist, in her weary-diner-waitress voice. She doesn't ask how I am. "I just finished the observation at Maresa's school," she says, "and I spoke with her teacher during recess. Are you aware of an incident a few weeks ago when Maresa ran and he chased her?"

I'm stumped, until the words "incident" and "chased" force their way into some sense with "Maresa ran."

"Oh! I forgot about that, yes, I am aware. The teacher told me right away. He —"

"Did you know that he picked her up and carried her back to the classroom?"

Yes, I did know.

"Are you aware that it's illegal to restrain a foster child?"

Well, he didn't restrain her, exactly, he just carried her back to the classroom. He's a very experienced teacher and —

"Are you aware that Maresa says that he twisted her arm? She says he hurt her."

Well, no. I mean, I'm surprised to hear that. The thing is, sometimes Maresa says *we're* hurting her, or shouting even when we're not, so even though she said that, I don't think . . .

"Do you restrain Maresa in your home?"

Well no, of course not, we . . .

"I'm sorry, but I have to report this. We'll need to have a team meeting about this incident as soon as possible. How is four p.m. today for you?"

Five

W<small>HAT THE APPLICATION SAID</small>: *Parent 1. Parent 2.*

"But we want to be equal parents."

"The woman has to be Parent One," the grey-crowned social worker said.

Among those dozen reasons I fell in love with you, Daddy, back when I thought of you only as Sebastian, here's #4: the collection of first-edition children's books in your bedroom.

In case you ever had a child to read them to, you said. Your favorite: *Heidi.*

I liked the idea of a man who wanted to read *Heidi* to his child. I liked the idea of raising a child with a man who made weird paintings of people with cities growing out of their heads.

The year before we met, I had quit dating a very charming, very affectionate man. Or rather, I had forced him to quit dating me. I was thirty-five and he was fifty, and he talked a lot, on our dates, about how glad he was he'd never had children. He asked if I'd go back on the pill, and I said no. I said if I got pregnant, I would want the baby. I said the taboo word. *Baby.*

I was surprised to hear myself say that, because I had always disliked the idea of being pregnant. But hormones and single-hood make for unfathomable vacillations. Even my childless-and-happy-about-it-now best friend had traversed her own season of longing. When she got a fertility test, wondering if her last chances were over at age forty-four, I went in for one, too. But apparently, by then, my hormones had swung back into the land of indifference.

"You're probably the first person the doctor's seen cheer at *that* test result," my best friend said. "So I guess that whole breakup thing was moot?"

But it wasn't. I was still glad to have moved on from Mr. No Kids.

What had I wanted that he couldn't give? Not *his* progeny, exactly, or mine. I wasn't one of those people for whom passing on genes was a necessary buffer to existential crisis. Existential crisis was bound to happen anyway. I'd already been through three. A flicker of one in junior high. A whopper of one in college. And a slow-burning one while married to my first husband, when Max spent long days at his office and I spent long days at home, taking lunch breaks to walk the abandoned dogs at the shelter, then going back to my desk and clipping death-joke cartoons out of *The New Yorker*.

These I posted on the refrigerator. A drawing of six men carrying a casket, and on the back of the casket, a bumper sticker: I'D RATHER BE LIVING.

"I guess writing a memoir about your dad dying in front of your eyes could make a girl a bit morbid," my then husband said, patting my head, and I refrained from admitting that the death obsession spiked right after I said "yes" to his marriage proposal.

Max was the one, back then, who believed in the necessity of kids. Said we had to have at least two. Not knowing I was Googling "abortion pill" every time the blood failed to flow.

I met him for lunch five years after the divorce. Admired pictures of his toddler daughter on his phone. His eyes were swollen and his hair thoroughly silver at forty-two. His girlfriend was insisting they have a second kid, he said. She wouldn't let it go.

"I'm glad we had Rosie, but —" He pointed to his hair. "This existential crisis stuff is still a bitch."

But you, Sebastian. You weren't looking to buffer existential crisis back when the art models' guild sent me, a stranger, to your class. Existential crisis is your natural state. Your favorite writer: Samuel Beckett. I stood naked and anonymous on that model stand as you exhorted your students to "look! Really *look!*" with the kindness of an uncle, though (as I'd later learn) several of the students complained you graded hard. That was one reason I fell in love, yes, your way with those students. Another: Your figure drawings featured thought bubbles. *Let's go. Yes, let's go,* your naked art models, standing contrapposto, were ruminating. *Nothing to be done.*

You were raised Episcopalian, baptized as a swaddling babe. I was raised nothing, baptized Episcopalian at twenty-five, a few months after I wandered into the cathedral on the hill. A recovering nihilist and a zealot for a confession of Christianity that was passionate about . . . paradox. "Church makes me uncomfortable," you said, but next to your bed hung a wooden crucifix carved in Ghana. You'd talked to Jesus, you said, back before your heart was diagnosed, before the surgery, those long nights when you were sure you were going to die. You showed me the conversation as you'd transcribed it. Jesus sounded an awful lot like Samuel Beckett.

Of course it's not as simple as saying I never wanted to be pregnant, is it? I *did* make a visit to the doctor after we married, inquiring about the latest technologies; everybody seemed to be doing it. A writing mentor of mine had just seen her forty-year-old daughter through the whole drill, recounted for me the howling breakdowns brought on by souped-up hormones, or maybe by dashed hopes and thwarted longing when the embryos didn't take — who could say?

I wasn't sure what I wanted the doctor to tell me. For years I'd run mental circles around the concept of God's will. The doctor foretold months of injections, slim statistical odds. One thing I knew: Whatever God's will was, this didn't feel like it.

Nothing to be done.

There is a certain freedom in that.

Private adoptions were too expensive. Babies from China were, too.

Nothing to be done.

Such coolness of decision-making, it would seem. And, really, why raise a child at all?

But then: the night you brought home the brochure you'd picked up at the neighborhood street fair where a foster agency had a booth. The children's faces. My limbs immobilized as my heart pumped hard.

Mysterious, the body's reasoning. Every sexual part of me burned. Not for the children, of course. For you.

And after the heat, when coolness again prevailed, we said to each other, What a solid reason to do this. To help someone. In the face of the unanswerable *why* of parenthood, we could stake ourselves on that justification. Too daunting to navigate the foster system alone. But with an agency behind us: maybe doable?

Now that the *thems* from the agency are proliferating, we divvy up the meetings 50–50. Our credo: Divide and conquer.

"Isn't your wife coming?" they ask when you show up solo for the appointment with the Family Support Specialist.

"Where's your wife?" asks the Home Certification Specialist.

"Your wife couldn't make it?" asks the leader of the fost-adopt support group.

I go to half the appointments alone, as we've agreed. Taking Maresa for sand-tray work with the blonde bimple therapist. Rendezvousing in the park with the grey-crowned social worker.

They never ask me where you are.

"The thing I realized is, the child is always going to need the mother more," my novelist friend says over breakfast the morning after his book tour appearance. A tattooed enlightened type from San Francisco, he feels guilty that his wife hasn't written much since giving birth.

Nature/nurture, I want to say. And: How conveniently nurture worked out for your writing life, my friend.

But there are upsides to being presumed Parent 1, yes. I like it when I tell Maresa we need to do some reading time and she comes to me with *Little Miss Spider.*

> *Little Miss Spider popped out of her egg*
> *Swinging down from a thread, she hung on by one leg . . .*
> *She decided to climb to the top of a tree*
> *Gazing out at the world, she sobbed, "Where could Mom be?"*

I read it to Maresa between deep breaths because I'm afraid when I get to Betty Beetle offering to help with the search, I'll cry.

I told the Family Support Specialist I didn't have time to come in the day she called about what's now termed "the school restraint incident." That was true, but another truth is that I wanted my husband with me. So here we are now, my love, as the blonde bimple therapist and her Family Support Skipper sit in separate straight-backed chairs, with us across from them on the couch, your palm spread on my spine.

"Wouldn't *someone* have had to pick Maresa up and bring her back to the classroom at some point?" I ask.

"Well," the blonde bimple therapist begins in her permanently worried voice.

"The point is that no emergency plan was in place," the Support Specialist says. "There should be a plan in place for such cases, so that the teacher calls the principal, or —"

"But wouldn't the *principal* then have to pick Maresa up and carry her back? Or if she keeps running, the policeman? I mean, *someone* would have to pick her up, right?"

Reason #8 I fell in love with you, Sebastian: Your hand on my back never means "stop talking."

The brunette Specialist makes nose-wrinkled eye contact with the blonde therapist, then turns back to me. "I'm not sure I see what you're getting at," she says.

When we walk out of the therapist's office, the grey-crowned social worker is waiting to take us back into her office. Convenient to have every team player in the same building, we'd once thought. One-stop shopping.

Paranoia involves intense anxious or fearful feelings often related to persecution, threat, or conspiracy.

A sensation Maresa must know. How could she not when we take her to the agency's cinderblock building, install her in the playroom with a VHS of *Sleeping Beauty*, then step into an office with strangers to discuss her fate?

The week before she moved in with us, one of the social workers from the far-off county made a special visit to the therapeutic foster home, picked her up for pizza and roller-skating. Last checkup before her big moving day.

We called Auntie that night for the update. "I don't know what happened, *strangest* thing. The social worker pulled up and Maresa just *instantly* started sobbing."

Maresa's teacher is one of the best in the district, we explain to the grey-crowned social worker, and the last thing we want to do is alienate ourselves from him. The whole school has been so good, we swear. They even have every teacher trained in the same Nurtured Heart techniques the Family Support Specialist has been teaching us! Honestly, this teacher has been a lifesaver.

Skepticism flickers across the grey-crowned social worker's face, and then she raises her eyebrows in the Look of Empathy.

"I'm surprised this teacher doesn't know the laws with foster kids, given all his years of experience. Really, you're doing him a favor here. Because I'd hate to see him in trouble with the law. You know, we want to keep *him* safe, too."

Twenty minutes later, we've negotiated reparations. Stood firm against her insistence that we alert the superintendent. We can meet with just the teacher.

"But call me afterwards to let me know he understood. It's very important that all the caretakers in Maresa's life are on exactly the same page."

This agency is big on two particular trademarked "approaches": Nurtured Heart and Beyond Consequences. Once upon a time, Sebastian, we read poetry together in our marital bed. Now: The Book. Black-and-white cover with a gold sticker that reads, *FREE BONUS: Two tickets to the Beyond Consequences, Logic, and Control workshop (worth $300 — details inside!).*

"Can I run this past you?" you say, flipping to your place as we lie in a state of disbelief that we've actually managed to get Maresa asleep.

You read aloud the "Parenting Example" about an adoptive mom struggling with "a defiant and rebellious 12-year-old." In a chart on the facing page is the "Traditional View," summarizing a "fear-based" response. Under this "paradigm," as The Book terms it, the mother doubles down on controlling her daughter. *She wakes up every morning and repeats her mantra of "I'm in charge; Rachel does not have the power to make me angry today."*

"Hmm," you say. "Well, we're definitely not learning the Traditional View."

You proceed to read aloud the "New View." The New View describes how the adoptive mother "implements the Stress Model" and realizes that the "intense anger" she's experiencing is "being driven from an unconscious place within her." *At this point, it is about Beth, not Rachel. The onus is on Beth to identify the source of her over-reactions to her daughter.*

Your Look of Perplexity is another one of the things I love most about you, Sebastian, so guileless. "So, I guess the New View is that you have to dig up some repressed trauma so that the onus is on you?"

During one of her last nights at her previous foster home, Maresa kicked a hole through a wall. Apparently she'd been sticking her feet in the other girls' faces, and when she got sent to her room she kept kicking, and then the drywall cracked.

"She'll have to pay for that out of her allowance," Auntie called and told us. "If she was one of my own, I'd paddle her. But of course they don't let you do that with these kids. It's a shame."

"Paddle her?!" I huffed after hanging up. "God, we've got to get that girl out of there." You warned me not to judge: Auntie was

doing a hard job, you said, harder than we probably understood.

So, weeks later, when Maresa began to tell us that Auntie
used to yell at her, that Auntie would make the girls get out of
the car and lie flat on the ground, that Auntie once slapped her
face, I said, "Oh, Maresa, honey, I'm so sorry that happened," in
a tone that implied grievous affront, while stopping just short
of condemning Auntie.

That was before I learned to dread Homework Hour. *Circle the
word in the puzzle, then read it aloud.* "So this one rhymes with
'cat,' but it starts with a 'b,' so that sounds like . . ."

"Stop it!" Across the room flies the pencil. "You're not *helping*
me!" Fists against table. "*Help* me!"

"I'm trying to, honey. So listen to these rhymes, okay? Cat,
rat, hat —"

"STOP!!!!" Fists flying at my chest.

I've been reading a book the agency didn't recommend, a book
our social worker hasn't heard of. A book by a neuroscientist
who studied trauma for forty years, focusing on the world's two
most dependably traumatized demographics: Vietnam veter-
ans and foster kids. *Limbic core. Amygdala. Medial prefrontal
cortex.* I cycle through these like rosary beads. *Top-down regulation versus bottom-up regulation.* But it still boils down to fight
or flight.

"She just hit me in broad daylight." That's what I say into your
voicemail, my love, because you're in San Francisco teaching,
unavailable to play good cop.

From down the hall as I'm still speaking into the receiver: *THUD THUD THUD* of foot against the wall.

But as I venture down the hall, the thudding stops. Maresa looking up from her bedroom floor with a glare. "Auntie used to shout at me," she says.

"I'm sorry, honey," I say.

"You don't sound *that* sorry."

Home seems to be getting worse, but at least school is getting better. She's stopped running off from the teacher. She comes home belting "Happy Days Are Here Again" and "Yellow Submarine." Among the many things we appreciate about Maresa's teacher is his taste in class sing-alongs.

Your electric piano stands dusty in the corner. The electric piano you accompanied me on back in your Mission Street flat when we fell in love. The piano you used to play every night after dinner. The one you stopped playing because Maresa can't restrain herself from adding avant-garde chords to your jazz improvisations.

You hear Maresa sing "Yellow Submarine" and you look at this piano like you've just been handed the keys out of the gulag.

"If I can get that sheet music from your teacher," you suggest to Maresa, "I can play it for sing-alongs right here at home. Fun, right?"

So we use the sheet music as our excuse to stop in and see the teacher after school. Don't mention a thing about the Family Support Specialist or the grey-crowned social worker; don't breathe a word about any notion of calling the superintendent. Just casually propose that since we'd come to get the music, maybe we should check in about Maresa's school behavior? Maybe make sure there's a plan in place in case she runs off like that again?

"Have you worked with many foster kids?" I ask, as though with idle curiosity.

"Dozens," the teacher says as we stand in the resource room, the copy machine's light slicing our abdomens.

"And how does Maresa seem..." I can't find acceptable words for what I'm trying to ask. "Comparatively?"

"Forceful," he says.

We call the grey-crowned social worker as we walk home with sheet music in hand. Oh, it went well, we tell her, *very* well. Oh *yes*, the teacher understands the protocol with foster kids now. Oh *of course* we were firm.

Maresa's spring break and your teaching spring break don't line up. Meanwhile, I don't get a spring break at all. But I can take my work anywhere, since I'm teaching retirees who want to write memoirs online this quarter. So: Divide and conquer.

Maresa and I drive to my mother's house in the Valley. Singing and car-dancing together to Ella Fitzgerald: *A-tisket, a-tasket, I lost my yellow basket.* Then Maresa says, "I want Kidz Bop!"

Auto-Tuned twelve-year-olds sing the sanitized rap songs. "Louder!" she squeals. "Louder!"

Two hundred and twenty-eight miles, four hours, I'm thinking: *SHUT UP SHUT UP SHUT UP SHUT UP PLEASE FOR A MOMENT SHUT UP.*

Time was, I couldn't suppress a groan at the seven-foot-tall iron gates that wall in my mother's complex. Now, though, I regard its features with a different eye. There's a playground at the center with everything rubber-padded. Like being locked inside a sanatorium. Which has its uses. Ahhhhhh.

"The surprising thing is," I explain on the phone to my blessedly blunt best friend, "how quickly the feelings bounce back. I mean, twenty minutes alone to recover, and the next sweet thing she does: You're in love again."

Case in point: That first night at my mother's house — guest room piled with freshly purchased toys, thanks be to God for eager new grandmothers — when Maresa wants to exercise with the Power Girl videos we found on YouTube. Hair in a black headband and face glistening like a four-foot-tall Rambo as she huffs, then pauses from running in place. "I have to write this all down!" Diary of a seven-year-old triathlete: *30 jumping jaks. Lunch fowad. Poosh Ups.*

And her voice in the bath, Lord — it's better than Calgon. Belting out "eeeee-yeah-ahs" like a baby Aretha Franklin. "Are you recording this?" Grandma Annie asks. I Facetime you in San Francisco so you can listen, but then Maresa comes out dripping wet and says, "Hi, Daddy!" And before I know it she's licking the screen and you're calling out, "Well, honey, good *night!*"

For bedtime reading, she's packed *Little Miss Spider.* Betty Beetle flies the baby spider around, asking all the other insects if

she's seen her mom, snatching baby spider out of the beak of a
bird who almost eats her alive.

> *Before she could blink she was whisked out of sight*
> *And brave Beetle Betty was hugging her tight.*
> *In her warm cozy home in the bark of a tree,*
> *The kind beetle asked, "Won't you stay here with me?"*

Maresa takes the big bed and I take the couch. In the morning, Sebastian, although I know you'd hate this, I give her Co-
coa Puffs.

Surfer dude social worker from the far-off county calls while
Maresa and Grandma are moving plastic pieces around a board
game that entails ruining everything your opponent's worked
for and then sarcastically saying you're sorry. *Shit*, I think as the
phone number flashes, and step outside.

"Hey!" surfer dude says. "So I heard about the meeting with
the teacher . . ."

I sputter about how the meeting with the teacher went so
well, how glad we are the agency had us *do* that. They're so
right, we want to protect Maresa and the teacher and we've got
to have an emergency plan in place. So we made 100 percent
sure the teacher understood the special laws about children in
foster care and —

"That's the thing," surfer dude says. "So, actually, there *are* no
special laws about teachers and foster kids."

Oh.

"I mean, if you think about it, that would be ridiculous,
right? The same laws apply to a teacher handling *any* child."

Oh.

"Can I level with you?"

Please. God, please — yes.

"The teacher didn't do anything wrong. Calling the super-intendent would be ridiculous. I mean, that agency was, like, *waaaay* out of bounds."

I'm less relieved than indignant. Biceps flexing.

But surfer dude goes on. "I didn't want to, like, put you and Sebastian in the middle, but since this came up, okay? We here at the county have a contract with *you*. That agency is supposed to work on *your* behalf, for *us*."

Hell yeah! But then surfer dude says something else: "*I'm* the one who makes the decisions about where Maresa will live."

Was it his future-tense phrasing that made my pulse speed?

There's also this: One of Maresa's former foster homes, so we learned during the disclosure meeting, was decertified. Brenda and Joe, their names were, the first foster parents to take in Maresa and her sister after the girls' mom went to jail. Brenda took them on hikes and picnics, Maresa has told us, and wore T-shirts with pictures of kittens. She's less nostalgic about Joe. We know from the disclosure reports that one night Maresa's sister had a panic attack and gulped down two dozen mela-tonin tablets, and that Brenda took her to the hospital. We know that the next week Brenda called in a seven-day notice for Maresa and her sister to be removed.

That morning with the disclosure worker, we'd asked why Brenda and Joe's home had been decertified.

"Oh, nothing egregious, they just had a different idea about the treatment plan" was all the disclosure worker would say.

⌒

What *Wounded Children, Healing Homes* says: *A person with a trauma history is not necessarily disqualified as a potential parent . . .*

Not necessarily.

What if, at some point, I need the grey-crowned social worker to have my back? She's the one in our town visiting us weekly, after all, writing reports to the far-off county. So even though surfer dude has granted me permission to ignore her, I think I'd better play nice. Better try again to finish The Book.

The Book's "New View" goes on to describe how the parent, Beth, stepped away from the fight with her foster daughter and "made space for her unconscious thoughts to surface."

Beth opens her eyes and exclaims out loud: "That's it! That's it!!!" Beth realizes that growing up with two alcoholic parents, she would always back down from arguments with her sister in order to keep peace in the home.

Beth realizes that now, as an adult, she is reenacting those moments. When her daughter argues with her, she is really seeing her sister.

Beth makes this associational connection so that the next time Rachel enters into an argument or talks back to her, Beth can acknowledge her unconscious desire to have the last word, which will then enable her to shift into a state of love with Rachel.

That's it! That's it! I try thinking to myself one day at my mother's house when Maresa begins throwing a ball in the hallway and I tell her she needs to do that outside and she says "No!" and I take the ball and she charges at me and says "Meanie! I HATE you! You *meanie!*"

I'm just intensely mad because Maresa's shouting reminds me of my abusive former stepfather! I'm just reenacting those moments from my own traumatic past! Now that I have made this associational connection, I shift into the state of unconditional love!

There's just one problem with this script.

I really don't think I'm any angrier than you would be in the same circumstances, Sebastian, and the most traumatic thing about your childhood is that one time your mother forgot to pack your peanut butter and jelly.

I am mad because a seven-year-old is attacking me.

Sorry, Freud, no dice.

Divide and conquer doesn't always match our individual strengths to the situation at hand. You're so good, Sebastian, at smiling and nodding and saying thank you and goodbye. Me, I blab. Spill my honest-to-God feelings. Call it the memoirist's curse. A spell of indiscretion that comes over me when my cordial husband isn't there to cast his influence.

The grey-crowned social worker says she needs to see me and Maresa the day after we get back from spring break. Mandatory report-taking and all.

She offers to meet in the park. I sit on a concrete curb beneath the monkey bars as Maresa swings like a banshee and debate whether warning her not to jump from the highest point will only firm up her resolve to do it. The problem being that the grey-crowned social worker is watching, and if I don't say anything, it'll look like I'm failing to keep Maresa safe.

I practiced my placid smile with you, Daddy, before leaving the house, and I think I'm holding it admirably as I tell the social worker about the trip to Grandma's, how Grandma and Grandma's husband, whom Maresa calls Papa, took Maresa to the zoo. The worker and I sit on the curb as the swing's chains creak. I've decided to say nothing about surfer dude's call about the teacher.

Perhaps the grey-crowned social worker is trying to make amends, too. "I'm sorry she can have a brusque tone," she says of the Family Support Specialist. And they hadn't realized I'd had such a busy workweek when they called us in for that meeting. But it really was important that we warn Maresa's teacher about working with foster kids, and —

"I really don't want to talk about the teacher again," I blurt.

Maresa swings higher and higher. I think about rising from the curb and warning her to be safe. Glance at the Easter basket full of candy the grey-crowned social worker has brought as a gift for my daughter. The grey-crowned social worker is always bringing gifts. Everyone is always bringing Maresa gifts. The way you and I took gifts to the other girls in Maresa's old foster home, I suppose, hoping to brighten their day with some small kindness. Envisioning their deprivations. Wanting them to like us. Wanting to feel we were helping.

I see now why Auntie seemed rather cool about our offerings.

The social workers bring gifts because they know their presence is "triggering."

The day after Maresa moved in, the grey-crowned social worker came by with a new backpack topped with a bow. Inside: school supplies and a stuffed giraffe. I remember looking at the giraffe and finding it a little random, a little disjunctive with the bunny theme we'd been building. I remember Maresa picking up the giraffe and asking, "Why did you bring me this?"

⌒

Maresa is swinging so high, the chain slackens before slapping tight again and creaking on the way down.

Before Maresa moved in, I used to walk two blocks down the street on Wednesdays for a forty-minute sit and dharma talk at the insight center. *Remember: Just like me, this person is doing his or her best,* reads the cheat sheet I stuck to the refrigerator.

"Are the nights getting better?" the social worker asks.

Not really, I say.

"I know it isn't easy."

Hopefully we'll get her past the panic attacks and sleeping before eleven soon, I say.

"Must be exhausting," the social worker says.

Well, it's just, when she screams at me — yeah, that's hard.

The grey-crowned social worker lights up at her chance to Connect, lifting her eyebrows into the Look of Empathy.

"Well, I imagine some of your own traumas get triggered."

Remember: Just like me, this person is . . . Fuck. Nirvana's a long way off.

"Maresa!" I call. Rise and play our game on the swings where Maresa sticks out her feet and I try to grab them and she giggles. "We better go home and make lunch," I say.

"And then I can have some more of the candy that the Easter Bunny brought?"

"Sure, honey. Now, say goodbye."

In the rearview mirror, I spot the grey-crowned social worker putting the extra Easter basket back in her car.

You're in the kitchen when we get home, Daddy, already grill-
ing Maresa's cheese sandwich. I groan and you flash me the sad-
clown look of sympathy, without even having to be told. Then
you put on the ear-to-ear smile for Maresa and call out, "*There's
my girl!*"

Not until a few months later will I find the *Virginian-Pilot* ex-
posé about the coauthor of The Book. It turns out the "adoption specialist" who electrified the social-work world with his
New Paradigm has been reprimanded by the Oklahoma state
licensing board for advertising himself with a diploma mill
PhD. He's a self-described entrepreneur who, in addition to
instructing adoptive families to drink from baby bottles at
the dinner table, hawks a paperback titled *Speaking and Selling to Skeptical Mental Health Audiences, Including How I Made
$21,300 in One Week of Public Speaking.* His methods had been
prescribed to a foster mom who was acquainted with another
family that, the article reports, still have nightmares about his
sessions. With this research in mind, the foster mom declined
to follow The Book's methods. The local foster services agency
removed her daughter from her home.

I will spend weeks writing an essay about The Book. I will sub-
title the essay "Coercion and the Foster Care System." Send it
to a longtime writer friend who is one of my most trusted first
readers.

   Methinks the narrator of this essay doth protest too much, she
will say.

Six

So for the first few months," the blonde bimple therapist says, "sounds like you three had a honeymoon."

Strange honeymoon. But then again, come to think of it, kind of like my honeymoon with my first husband. I couldn't sleep next to Max, either. From the moment I said "yes" to our last night in bed together, I just lay paralyzed, mind racing. *What is wrong with me that this doesn't feel right?*

When you come to our bed at midnight, fierce Little One, my body reacts in ways I can't unwill. If only I could lose consciousness. But even if you lie still — not likely — my heart speeds. Five nights in a row, there you are, stumbling through the black, sucking your thumb. "Goosebumps," you say into the dark, and I'm thinking *shit*, because how can I say no? But Daddy is firm. Oh no no no no no, he says, lifting you out of bed and carrying you back down the hall.

The friend I've made in town, an actress with two sons, says it's a shame the foster care system makes everyone nervous. "I mean, if you weren't worried about being under surveillance, you'd go ahead and let her sleep with you, right? Cody slept with me until he was nine."

But Auntie keeps an ironclad rule for all the foster girls in her house. "Oh good Lord no," she says. "Can you imagine? I'd just lie there with my eyes open, flipping out."

The bright moments tend to come in the daytime. So many of them that I fill a notebook, like a newlywed cherishing fleeting sweetness. Like the day when we ask if you want to go with me to the laundromat or stay home with Daddy.

"But if I *go* I'll miss Daddy! But if I stay I'll miss *you!*"

And you're not a child doll, you're a *person*, with a mix of talents that intoxicate us.

"Look at that!" Daddy said, open-mouthed over your tempera rendering of a snowman framed by piney hillsides. "Maresa, how did you know how to *do* that?"

Turning to me, the former full-time artist's model who, despite sitting in on hundreds of lessons, still draws stick figures. "Look at that! That's atmospheric perspective!"

It wasn't just your athleticism and your singing and your art skills that beguiled.

On our second visit to get to know you, back in Auntie's town, we took you to the roller-skating rink. You raced around that rink so madly, in such a frenzy of determined fun, that the roller-rink ref in his black-and-white-striped jersey had to keep coming and blowing his whistle. And yet: The moment another kid fell, you stopped, raced back, and knelt to help that kid up. Every time.

"She's got a good heart," Daddy said.

I'd already figured that. Then again, I'm predisposed to see a gift for art as a mark of moral character. Reason #2 I fell in love with Daddy: I liked his art. And not just in the sense that I thought it was pleasant enough to look at, or showed skill. I was modeling ten or twelve gigs a week back when I met Daddy, all over the Bay Area for all kinds of groups, and often when someone's drawing or painting flattered me, I was tickled. Daddy started showing up at various community drop-in sessions — to see me? I wondered — but his drawings never flattered. I'm looking at one he made the day we met, in fact, as I write this. In it, I'm standing contrapposto, and my thighs, which at that time, to my pride, were quite slender, look like the haunches of a draft horse. But I could look at that drawing all day. There's something true about it.

You weren't as into your ballet classes as that CHILDREN AVAILABLE flyer promised. I had to bribe you to pull on the tights. You broke out into cartwheels during the piqués. And then, the moment we'd walked out of the studio: "Do I *have* to go back?"

On the other hand, we can't keep you away from the art supplies. Immediately after school you're taking out the watercolors, the acrylics. Coloring books offend. You make a painting featuring a red block with wing-like shapes attached, blue curves floating all around like parentheses. It could be a bird, or a totem figure. You look sorry for me when I inquire about your subject matter. "Art is what you *see* in it, Mommy."

Daddy hangs it above his desk, next to his own paintings.

"Better than I could do," he says bittersweetly.

I could look at it all day.

You're an artist, we've told you, and you've taken to carrying a sketchbook everywhere. The kids at school — the kids you claim yell at you and hate you — give you their milk money so you'll draw their portraits.

What you're not: a girly girl. The garage filling with dolls and dresses inventoried for a future garage sale. "Really, she *hates* Barbies," we explain to all the kind friends who send gifts, "and she absolutely will *not* wear pink," but they don't see how that can be true.

It's a good match, they say. She's got love for art in common with Daddy, and love for singing with Mommy.

But we think mostly of you speeding around that roller-skating rink like a NASCAR champ on meth. I imagine an alternative online dating universe for foster kids and would-be parents.

Interests: Art-making, singing, reckless adrenaline-seeking.

Would eHarmony have an algorithm for that?

On the phone with practically everyone I know, I'm like one of those dolls you hate — push the button on my back and I'll say the same phrase.

We can't wait for you to meet her!

We can't wait for you to meet her!
We can't wait for you to meet her!

The most excited of the excitables was your new grandmother, my mother. Which made me so grateful I ached, which made it impossible to say no when Grandma Annie asked if she could come meet you back in December, the weekend of your very first pre-placement visit.

"But maybe . . . just come meet us at church?" I said to my mother, thinking that might be less pressure on you. "You could just . . . see her for a bit at the coffee hour?"

And so my mother raced up Route 80 just as she'd sped to the hospital the day my brother's first child, your cousin, was born. Four hours from the Valley to here. For twenty minutes in a crowded parish hall.

It's beyond shameful to me now that I disliked Grandma Annie's husband when she married him, twelve years ago. A big-bellied Kentucky native with a thing for little girls. No funny stuff, mind you, just guilt: He left his own daughter to be raised by his first wife when she was six, and hardly saw her; she's now a meth addict who pointedly doesn't send Father's Day cards.

Before you even visited, the man you now call Papa Tim bought the first gift: a contraption called Rainbow 'Round My Room. Spent an hour wrangling the battery compartment until that thing projected a perfect arc of colors above your future bed. He's confident with kids because he has a granddaughter he sees every weekend; he would have adopted her if his meth-addict daughter had let him.

He looked up at the red-orange-yellow-green-blue and clucked. "Yep, this little girl's life's about to get a lot better."

I remember how he strode right up to you after communion, as the line stalled between the church and the parish hall.
 "Hey there, little girl — I think we better call the *police!*"
 Your face falling off a cliff before he could finish the joke. Like a man with a badge might actually be coming to handcuff you that minute.
 And then, Papa Tim pushing on with the punch line. "'Cause it looks like *some*body stole your two front *teeth!*"

Grandma Annie whispered to me, as you hoarded Oreos from the hospitality table, "I'm sorry, I *told* him to hang back and keep his mouth shut!"
 But I was thinking, *Please, just tell me you'll keep sending the Legos and the Jelly Bellies and the skorts. Dear God, please, just tell me you'll come back.*

They came back three weeks after you moved in, took a room at a bed-and-breakfast down the street, came over nightly to play Connect Four and Go Fish. To honeymoon along with us.
 "Alrighty girl," Papa Tim said when it was all done, "you keep your nose dry until next time, you hear me? Now come give your papa a hug."
 And you threw your arms around his belly, then stepped back, looking at me with a wrinkled nose like you'd caught a bad smell.
 "Um, Papa is *really* fat," you announced.
 Next time, Grandma Annie came alone.

⌒

Was it a honeymoon? Or more like dating? The way that dating is a relentless audition? Except half the time, you don't seem to know whom you're auditioning for. Have you been at this so long, you'll play to anyone who's listening?

Saying to grocery store cashiers, "I'm different for a kid. I don't like sugar. *Really!* Guess what my favorite food is. *Spinach!*" By March I've seen you perform this act so many times that I know your next move: turn to everyone behind us in line and shout, "One time I ate spinach for *dessert!*"

Daddy is all too eager to believe the advertising and serves you spaghetti sauce involving spinach and onions and fresh basil. You said "Yum!" the first three times he served it. Then, in early March, you let a green glob hang from the tine. "What's this?"

Your favorite food, we explained.

"I only like spinach not hot. And with ranch."

Daddy rolled his eyes. "Honey, she's *seven*," I said, walking over to the fridge to fetch you fresh spinach, setting it out with a ramekin of the ranch dressing I bought specially for you the week before.

"This ranch tastes funny."

"There's *nothing* wrong with it," Daddy said.

At which you jumped up from the table, ran screaming as though pursued by snakes, and slammed your bedroom door. *THUD. THUD. THUD. THUD. THUD.*

"Honeymoon's over," Daddy said.

The Family Support Specialist sent us a link to a video advertising trainings in Nurtured Heart techniques. In one section of the video a man stands on a backyard deck with a barrel-

chested teenager who is tapping his fist against a window while
wailing like an abused dog.

"I see you *want* to smash the window, but you're *not*," the
man says in a voice like Mr. Rogers's. "I see you're doing a *great*
job. I see you taking a deep breath and making *good decisions*.
You *want* to smash that window, but you're not doing that, *are*
you?"

The other technique, which the blonde bimple therapist taught
us, is "mirroring the feelings." In the office alone with me, the
white-noise machine whirring, she instructed, scrunching her
forehead and flaring her eyes like a gorilla: "You seem ANGRY.
Are you REALLY ANGRY?" Then, in a quicksilver change
that could give Marcel Marceau a run for the money: "Now you
seem *saaaaaad. I see that you're soooo, soooo saaaaaad.*"

I came to your room with a peanut butter and jelly sandwich.

THUD. THUD.

Thud.

"I can see that you *really* want to kick a hole in that wall, but
you're not. I see you making a great decision."

"STOP IT!"

THUD.

"You look *reaaaaaally* ANGRY. I can see that you're AN-
GRY."

"Why are you TALKING to me that way?"

The next night, Daddy made macaroni and cheese. Not from
a box, no — he has his principles. And his mother's recipe.
Which prompted you to ask for seconds.

Reason #4 I fell in love with Daddy: the photo of his parents I spotted hanging next to his desk the day I first came over to sing a few songs while he played the piano. I had never known a man who kept a picture of his mom and dad next to his desk.

They were a factor in our choosing this town in the foothills. We could live just a ten-minute drive from them. Sunday dinners and all. Which, truth be told, weren't that comfortable for me: the lace runners, the cane-backed chairs, the rack of lamb perfected through decades of no-career mothering. And Daddy's father at the head of the table, barking like Archie Bunker.

For that delicate first meeting, Little One, we took you over for lunch. Something kid-friendly, we'd requested. There were finger sandwiches and tomato soup in a gilt-edged tureen.

I remember the silence, the glare of the oak floors. Daddy's mom at one head of the table and Daddy's dad at the other, and there we were in the middle, Little One, both of us unnaturally upright, with silk napkins on our laps, and all I could think was *I have to get her out of here I have to get her out of here I have to get her out of here.*

In the car, as we three-point-turned out of the driveway, I found out Daddy felt the same. "*That* was strange" was all he said, for the moment, with you right there in the back seat.

"We were just nervous," his mother explained.

The next time we went over for dinner, Grandma Elsie made a special point of asking you if you wanted to light the candles, which of course thrilled your pyro-fascinations to no end.

You blew out the match, ran into the living room, and began

catapulting yourself from the peach sofas, babbling and singing, like a patient off her lithium.

"Is her brain messed up or something because her mother
did drugs?" Grandpa Bob barked at Daddy, loud enough for
you to hear.

Know what's funny, Little One? I did the same thing the first
time *I* went over to Grandma and Grandpa's house. It was just
after Daddy and I had decided that he'd move with me to North
Carolina, when we'd known each other all of three months. We
knew we were going to marry when we got there, but we were
still keeping it all mum. When we drove up to his parents' and
walked in and I saw that table so immaculately set, something
coiled tight in my gut like a spring.

"Phew!" I shouted, not five minutes through the door. "That
was a long drive! I need to get a bit more exercise before dinner if you don't mind." And then, I kid you not, Little One, I
launched into mad jumping jacks and push-ups right there in
the living room.

What do you want us to have her call you? we asked.

Grandma and Grandpa, they told us.

Grandma Elsie takes pride in the finer touches. When we visited on St. Patrick's Day, she'd cooked corned beef, and there
were shamrocks and cards at each place setting. *I've got the luck
o' the Irish to be with you!* your card read, and you had a special basket full of green candies and a green pen with a giant
green clover on the cap. Also: knitting needles. And then, after
it was all over, after the homemade strawberry shortcake, you

didn't catapult off the couches, bless you, but sat down next to Grandma and let her teach you how to cast on.

"I'm knitting a kitten hammock!" you told me a few weeks later, as you held up your handiwork. "Like, if you found a tiny kitten in the street, and you took it in and tried to make it feel better? You could put it in the hammock like this and rock it like a baby . . ."

After the blue kitten hammock, your next product was a long strip of green stitches, bulging in the middle like a snake that just ate lunch.

A scarf? I asked.

"No!" you said. "A tie. For Grandpa Bob."

And soon enough, there was Grandpa Bob sitting at the head of the table, straightening his green tie like a dapper gent. "She made this, can you believe it? Not bad, kiddo, not bad."

Another cool thing about you: You can swim. Your Court-Appointed Special Advocate taught you, so we're informed. She visited you once a month when you lived with Auntie, and she'll keep visiting even now, until we finalize, but having spent the winter in Mexico, she missed our honeymoon. The day she first comes to our house, the day I first meet her, you wake up angry. Won't put on your shoes. The knock on the door comes just as you're screaming, "STOP IT!!!! NO! YOU MEANIE!"

She's a tall, solid woman in her fifties, I'd guess, and her face as I open the door is like stone. I'd been looking forward to meeting her, because a friend of mine also volunteers as a CASA, and because she's known you since you were five. I'd been hoping she'd tell me about your past. But when she steps into the house I remember that in a few months she'll write a report to file with the judge.

"Sounds like a rough morning," she says with the inflection of a prison warden.

"Well, she's got her swimsuit on!" I say. Her face unchanging. Until you jump up and hug her, shouting, "Mary! Swimming!"

At her hotel, you plunge into the deep end, even though the pool isn't heated, swimming all day until she returns you to us with raisin fingertips.

It's April now. Another package sent by Grandma Annie on our doorstep. Turquoise tankini, size 7/8. Shoes made of mesh, size 1.

I hope these fit! She'll need them for the waterslide park! Papa and I are counting down. Can't wait!!!!!!

Daddy flinches at the sight of the open Lands' End box. "I hope this won't prove regrettably ambitious."

Seven

THE ENTIRE FAMILY *can find the perfect combination of fun and relaxation on seven acres of thrilling aquatic recreation.*

The entire family: forty-two descendants of Grandma Annie's mother, i.e. my grandmother, i.e. your new great-grandmother. Whose descendants include my three aunts. Their husbands. Nine cousins. Eighteen second cousins. Various other people I am reportedly, in some fashion, connected to. And my brother — your new uncle — and his wife and two kids.

Confession: I hate family reunions. My formative family unit, after the night of the blood and the gurney and my father in the morgue, comprised just three: your grandma Annie, your uncle (my younger brother), and me. "Oh, *and* the sociopath addict stepfather I made you live with until you were thirteen," Grandma Annie would remind me, out of guilt, if she could hear. But I don't need her to pay any more penance. She kicked him out eventually. She did her best.

Daddy's the one who extols extended kinship. He's right, I know, but I just can't hack it. At *his* last family reunion, the summer before we found your picture in the binder, he circulated around every single picnic table, inquiring about Uncle Jim's Costa Rica trip and Aunt Nellie's bingo nights with the relish of a celebrity hound. While I complained of migraine.

"If this was *your* family, you'd want to stay," Daddy said. But he was wrong. My family, I'd have left an hour earlier. Less chance of leaving grist for gossip.

Relax with comfort fare and libations amidst the sounds of soothing waves at The Oasis Bar and Grill, located inside Arizona's premier water adventure.

Since we've got weeks to prepare, your daddy and I bone up with some of the actually useful books we've found. The name of the game, evidently: High-Nurture, High-Structure Parenting.

Natalie and John have lived in their present home for eight months. Birth siblings, they have both experienced multiple placements and have an emotional age of about three and four. In fact, they are six and seven.

As they enter a picnic area for a potluck with their parents and some friends, their parents tell them how happy they are to be with them . . .

Mom says, "First we will eat while you get used to the group. Then Natalie will go with Dad, and John will go with me down to the play area. The rules are, number one, stay close enough that a parent can touch you; and number two, have a good time with your family. We love you!" . . .

While this seems like a lot of effort, it contrasts positively with

*a scenario in which the children are migrating to other picnic sites,
grazing from strangers' tables, and ignoring their frantic parents.*

Grandma Annie: "C'mon, how much trouble can she get into
at a waterslide park? The lifeguards are *everywhere*. She'll be
having so much fun!"

It's Grandma Annie who books the double-queen suite and
pays for it. Grandma Annie who buys the airline tickets. Your
first flight.

"Oh, dear," the grey-crowned social worker says. "I don't
want to throw a wrench in your plans, but you know, you can't
travel with a foster child over state lines."

Actually, we'd already called surfer dude to check. He autho-
rized us to take you anywhere within the continental United
States.

"That's . . . surprising," the grey-crowned social worker says
with a face that reminds me of the only grade school teacher
who actively disliked me.

"Everyone at school hates me!" So you've been saying for five
months. January through April, I walked over to the school
at many a recess to check out this claim. Stuck the VISITOR
sticker to my chest and stood on the blacktop urging you to
hula-hoop or get in line for two-square.

What I saw: Kids calling, "Hey, Maresa, come try this! Hey,
Maresa, what're you up to? Hey, Maresa, wanna play?" While
you crawled on your belly to hide beneath the slide.

And every morning: "Noooooo! I don't WANT to go to
school!" Twenty-one unexcused tardies, the notice from the

school district says, directing Daddy and me to explain ourselves to the superintendent.

Then, in June, inexplicably, your tune changes. "I wish school
wasn't ending. I *love* school!"

*Whether meeting with colleagues or vacationing with friends, gra-
cious service, creative culinary delights, and unique recreational activities await. All in the midst of a tropical escape.*

Hat: *check.* Steel water canteen: *check.* Triple-digit SPF: *check.*
Not that any of it will help Daddy much. *Here, try a little heat
and sun with your atrial septal fatigue!* One hundred and four-
teen in Phoenix, the global warming Cassandras are shouting.

Daddy's been dizzy a lot lately, and it's only eighty-five here in
the foothills. The spells tend to come after he's tried to help
you with questions on your math sheet and you've stabbed his
arm with a pencil. Or just after you've begged him to play "sack
of potatoes," when he hoists you over his shoulder and walks
around calling, "Where should I set down this sack of potatoes?" as you cry out with joy. Until you cry with something
else. Oh, those living room games. From *Romper Room* to *One
Flew Over the Cuckoo's Nest* in three point five seconds.

Sometimes I find Daddy collapsed on the bed and his flesh
looks so ashen and I say a one-word prayer and I watch his
wrist for a pulse.

*Resort guests are invited to stay cool in the shade while kicking back
poolside in a private Oasis Cabana.*

There are mist generators. Pineapple slices cut in the shape of daisies and lanced like shish kebabs. Bottles of Aquafina that crackle as your cousins suck the contents down.

Their mothers, my cousins, are lathering sunscreen onto compliant backs. While you shout, "*Stop* it, Mommy!" Stomping off with the one white streak I managed slashed like war paint across your scapula.

I attempt the Lazy River with you, envisioning us each in one hole of the two-person raft. "STOP following me, Mommy!" So I retreat to the cabana, where reclines Uncle Phil, pale and blitzed and trembling as ever — he never did seem to enjoy having six kids, even now that they're grown. Cousin Holly is there, too, with her two grade-schoolers flicking eight-dollar slushies in each other's faces. And in the corner sits my cousin Melanie, always the quiet, shy one three decades ago, when we were dashing naked down Slip 'N Slides together. Her daughter Lula is eight now. About your age. Quiet, like her mom. Eating yogurt off the spoon her mom holds up to her mouth, then chirping like a baby bird. "Mommy, let's go in the wave pool together!"

The waterslide park is circled by a ten-foot-high fence, like a giant carbon-spewing aviary.

"I think I've got another hour in me before I melt," Daddy says, then heads off to attempt joining you on a ride.

I stare hypnotized by Melanie and Lula in the wave pool. Up and down they bob on the waves, up and down, like seagulls resting on the surface of the ocean, and my eyes start to water and my throat constricts on a chunk of flower-fruit. *Focus on the waves, up and down, up and down . . .*

"Looks like you need this," teetotaling Mormon Uncle Phil says, handing me a beer.

But I decline, returning to the suite sober to log in to my class. A dozen women smile back across the video feed, just as scheduled. Barbara is writing about being a sheep rancher in Montana. Elena posted a chapter about caring for her passive-aggressive bipolar mom. Christina shared an essay about being abused by her father.

The week's lesson is Point of View. How a writer has much more license for imagining other characters' experiences than she may think, even when writing from real life. How exercising such empathy can transform a story from a pity party into a spiritual reconciliation with reality.

The air conditioning clicks on and hums. The faces on the screen are listening so intently. The shutters in this suite are so straight and symmetrical.

"IT HUUUUUUURTS! IT HUUUUUUURTS!"

"Think we got a little too much chlorine!" Daddy says, dashing after you, closing the bedroom door. The wall no match for your screams.

Apologies to the faces on the screen. Promises to make up for it all by reading more pages.

"OOOOOOUUUUUUUCCCCCCHHHH!"

Focus on the waves, up and down, up and down . . . "Oh, my poor sweetie," I say. Applying eye drops bought at an extortionist's rate from the gift shop. Strapping on goggles. "Now we've got you all fixed up! But listen, you need to stay hydrated."

You spit the water clear across the room. "This tastes gross!"

I can't deny that the tap water here contains top notes of laundry detergent and chlorine. All the better, no doubt, for selling those $4 Aquafinas and $6.50 Diet Cokes.

Thankfully, Uncle Phil's got a cooler full of free soda pop at the poolside barbecue that night. At least the scene is a break from the waterslide "adventure." Just the family fenced in here with the hotel pool. Your uncle, my brother, is in the shallow end with your toddler cousins and a Corona. Tattooed pecs permanently pumped from two tours to Iraq.

"Yo, sis, where the hell's Sebastian?"

I explain that your daddy needed a rest.

"What? That wimp. Get him on out here!"

Who knew my husband was so popular? "Where's Sebastian?" everyone asks between water somersault contests, between shoulder-mounted games of chicken, between races to touch the bottom, which you win. "Where's that reclusive husband of yours?"

To which my brother adds: "And why weren't *you* in the cabana this afternoon, sis? Wait, don't tell me. Work. Right? Yeah, you've always got work."

"Oh, we tried foster kids, too," my six-foot-tall aunt Delia is saying, as her husband, Uncle Phil, flips the burgers. Their oldest son, my cousin Rick, is in the deep end with his two teenage girls from his first marriage; his second marriage just ended because he lost his job, slapped his wife, and was diagnosed bipolar, or so I learned while Uncle Phil was out of earshot in the cabana. Phil and Delia's three other sons' diagnoses are familiar to me from years of phone calls with my grandmother, who always shares the information with an "oh dear" or a "heavens to Betsy": Tyler, ADD; John, OCD; Kevin, BPD.

But then there's the youngest, shy Melanie. Holding her daughter Lula on her lap in the hot tub as the surface undulates.

You are so much cuter in my eyes, fierce Little One. Just look at you in your turquoise tankini, your brown limbs so solid and strong. When your face is wet, those dimples shine. And your front teeth are coming in so straight. Later, I'll print the photo your uncle, my brother, took of you on this night. The picture of you with hair slicked and dripping, chin held high. You look to me like a first-grader-sized Olympian who just won the swim meet. I will set this photo atop my bookcase, next to the photo of me and Daddy on our first anniversary. While you're at school, I'll gaze upon it.

"You can't catch me!" you say as I get into the pool. You're right. And I don't want to repeat what half the family just saw — the splash you aimed with a sniper's precision at my face.

"Stop being such a priss, sis," your uncle says, and aims the next splash.

What the actually useful book warned us about High-Nurture, High-Structure Parenting: *People usually pair high structure with low affection in our society . . . A challenge for parents is enduring the reaction that some people have to structure. Outsid-*

*ers may believe that if the parents simply relaxed, then their child
would not have a problem.*

Me: "Maresa, sweetie, remember the rule about running on the
concrete?"

Your uncle, with a swig of Corona: "Sis, chill out."

Me: "Maresa, honey, it's eight p.m. Time to get out and start
our bedtime routine."

Your uncle: "Jesus, sis, it's *vacation.*"

That night, everything's okay. It's the next night, the final night,
the night *after* you stand atop the raft on the Lazy River and
spit at the lifeguard. *After* you claw my grip off your wrist and
charge to the top of the Depth Plunge. *After* all the families
bicker over which clans will go to dinner where, and who should
pay. *After* Aunt Holly says just forget it and drives back to California with her kids a day early. *After* Aunt Melanie and Lula
join us at the restaurant where the waiter does magic tricks at
the table and Papa Tim eats a full rack of ribs and Grandma
Annie sticks her tongue out with you in the photo booth. That
final night, when we've survived your uncle ordering everyone
around for the big group photo, when my head is forgetting
the whack from the patio umbrella. ("Well, get out of the way,
didn't you see me coming?") That very last night, when we're on
the home stretch, or so I thought.

That final night, I indulge in a Corona after dinner, poolside
with the aunts and uncles. Sip and ponder the question everyone's asking: "So how's it going with Maresa?"

The memoirist's curse possessing me.

"Okay, honestly? It's hard." Ah, Corona, as if loose lips need abetting. "A lot of the time it's really hard." Another sip. "The thing is, it's taking a toll on Sebastian's health. That's why he's been resting in our room. Sometimes when she screams — I don't know if his heart can take it."

"Do what you have to do to protect yourself," Aunt Delia says, shoulders and voice rising. "God *knows* we tried with our foster kids."

At which, ninety-five-year-old Great-Grandma Doris cranes her neck from the lounge chair.

"Don't tell me you're sending her *back?!*"

Who knew that a ninety-five-year-old's Oklahoma drawl could blast through chatter like a train whistle's scream?

Awww, do you really have to get her to bed so early? everyone's asking Daddy. It's vacation! Have a sugar cookie! Here, take the extras back to your room. Here, how about some sodas? Dr Pepper? It's vacation!

Divide and conquer: Daddy will get your bedtime routine rolling. I'll put in a bit of face time with each relative, then meet you and Daddy at the suite in time for a chapter of *Stuart Little*.

Our Deluxe Resort Suites feature a preferred location close to the Oasis Water Park and come complete with one king or two queen beds, a private balcony or patio and separate living room with queen sofa bed. An oversized work area with high-speed Internet access offers an atmosphere perfect for work or planning the next day's activities.

⌒

Also offered by the "oversized work area": a desk with solid wood legs perfect for bashing one's head against.

Which is what you're doing right now, Little One. Your beautiful brown little forehead. The square table leg.

"I HATE YOU! GO *AWAY!*"

I'm not sure how we got to this moment.

Just as I'm not sure how, back with the man who became my first husband, I ended up screaming, "YOU DON'T LOVE ME! I DON'T *NEED* YOU!" and raising my hand to slap him at 2 a.m. in a hotel room the night before his brother's wedding.

You were complaining about the taste of the tap water, Little One, that much I recall. Saying we had to find your water bottle, which you'd left at the waterslide park. Saying if we couldn't find the water bottle, you needed a soda. Which Daddy flat-out refused.

And then you were banging your head against the desk leg and your eyes were like a caged animal's and your forehead was bleeding.

I was swabbing you with a cool washcloth and you were batting away my arms and screaming.

As Daddy lay in the other room. Staring up at the ceiling.

You wouldn't stop batting away my arms. You wouldn't stop screaming. You were saying things you'd regret. I was saying things I'd regret. "Maresa, please. We can't *do* this, Maresa. We just can't *do* this. You have to work with us, or — we can't *do* this."

And then I was leaving you screaming on the sofa. Abandoning you for Daddy in the bedroom.

I closed the door. Watched his wrist for a pulse. Knelt next to the bed. Pressed my cheek to his chest. Felt beating like a machine gun's fire.

Sebastian. My lamb. Salty wet face, closed eyes. Writhing side to side. Murmuring, "I'm sorry, honey, I'm so sorry." As the screams in the front room keep coming. "It's my fault. I'm just . . . weak. We can't help her because I'm too weak."

It's not your fault, I'm saying, it's not your fault, but he doesn't hear. And then his chest is heaving against my cheek, and the sound we are making is called a sob.

Eight

THE PHOTOS ARE going up on Facebook.

Cousin Rick with his teenage daughters: *Family rocks!*

Cousin Holly, apparently regretting her early flight home: *Best vacation EV-ah!*

A text from Grandma Annie while we're at baggage claim — *I feel like I'm mourning.*

— *We didn't say we're giving up. We're just saying it's difficult.*

— *I know. I just couldn't stop crying on the drive home, and your brother . . .*

— *What did you say to him?!*

The flight home, the drive from the airport — we move as though ferrying a vial of plutonium. Swaddle you in your blankie. You suck your thumb, which I rarely see you do. And then, when we walk in our door, "There's no place like home!" you exclaim, your eyes bright like Dorothy's. You sleep twelve hours.

Then wake up and detonate.

"I DON'T WANT TO EAT! I DON'T WANT TO

GET DRESSED! GO AWAY, YOU MEANIE. GO AWAY,
YOU'RE *RUDE!*"

"Listen, sis," your uncle is saying the next day as I gaze out the
bedroom window at the garden. Thinking, *Go figure, the toma
toes are taking off this year.* "I'm gonna level with you, because
I love you. You've just gotta suck it up, you know? Parenting
ain't easy. I mean, there's been times. Braden grabbed my razor blade from the shower, almost shoved it in his mouth,
I'm thinking, shit, I let him get his hands on that, I'm a fucking failure. Oh, and screaming! You think *you're* dealing with
screaming? I'm living with a fucking two-year-old. *I'll* tell you
about screaming. And so here's the thing, sis: You gotta just
SUCK IT UP."

Yes, yes, I say, but the difficult thing is, Sebastian gets weak.

"Now come on, is he really *that* weak, or is he just —"

He has a heart defect!

"Yeah, and they fixed it. I mean, that shit doesn't get you off
the hook, sis."

It's a medical condition!

"So you're gonna throw a pity party? Hey, I'll be honest with
you. Sometimes Maria comes to me for pity, and I don't have
it. You know? I mean, if Seb can't commit, you tell him, 'Well,
that's your choice, dude. There's the door.'"

Well, I don't handle my marriage that way.

"Yeah, well, good luck."

Two things that haunt me, Little One, as I write this. Two
things that give the lie to the notion that I'm really writing this
to you, because why would I ever tell you this? Except to ask
your forgiveness. Except to admit that yes, if I could go back, I

would do things differently, I would. Except to admit the possibility that I failed you.

Your uncle's observation: "I can see that she wants really badly to be close to you, if you'll just let her."

And what I wrote in my journal that afternoon, in the garden:

If we don't carry on, I know Sebastian will blame his health. I wonder if I'll reach for that excuse, too, or if I'll have the humility to confess that no, it was me — I couldn't handle any more.

I wonder if I'll be honest: I chose my husband, my quiet life of garden and books.

What the social workers all say: Most fost-adopt families have to go through a crisis.

— *And then what?* Grandma Annie writes back when I text her this.

— *I guess either they carry on or they don't.*

"Ooooh, perfect timing!" Auntie gasps on the speakerphone. "She'll be back with all the girls for the parade and the fireworks!"

Four days, three nights. Respite care, we're calling this. You bounce with glee as though the water park escapade never happened.

"This'll give you and Sebastian some rest," Auntie says. "I'm sure you could use it!"

Oh, blessed NRA-card-carrying woman. Feathery blonde hair like an angel's wings. She'll even meet us halfway, at the Krispy Kreme parking lot.

⌒

The drive with you in the back seat, babbling to Kidz Bop. Counting down the miles till I drop you off. Thinking, *God, if I can just drop you off, I can be human again.*

But in the Krispy Kreme lot I'm longing for a last glance at the curve of your dimples.

"Give me one more kiss, huh?" I say. "And have fun! Remember, Auntie has my number. You can call me and Daddy anytime."

"Why would I do that?" you say with perfect innocence, and race to the Durango.

Your Mother's Day card stares from the refrigerator when I walk back into the house. Drawn at school, laminated by your teacher. It nearly made me cry the day you brought it home, though I felt uneasy, too, about my delight. It took Daddy's sleuthing skills to figure out that *My mommy likes pees meetings* meant "My mommy likes peace meetings." Where you got that phrase I'll never know, but when I asked, you explained that you meant sitting on the carpet and meditating together.

Now I understand what made me uncomfortable: You were forced to write it.

Nine

We're alone.

Here's something I loved from my single years — the years, that is, that followed my divorce from Max. I loved coming back to my apartment after a day of art modeling and a quick stop into Whole Foods for takeout and Pinot Gris, loved riding the elevator up from the garage, walking alone into that studio apartment. The cat curled on the pillow. The moonlight slanting through the open window at the far end of the kitchen. The stillness of the night outside as I walked, *click click click*, on kitten heels across oak floors.

Our house is quiet like that now.

On the first day we work in the garden. The tomato plants chest-high. So much fruit, green and tiny and tantalizing. Unbelievable. A little seedling became that.

On the second day we walk Bourbon Hill. Observe the bees on the clematis and the calendula. Spot Steller's jays in the pines.

Take sandwiches to the river. Read art biographies and poetry as rainbow trout flicker in the shallows.

There is so much time. It is as spacious as the quiet.

At least for two more days.

Days like our honeymoon. That weekend after our appointment with the judge, we lay beneath the elm in front of the old stone house with the windowless attic that the college in North Carolina had deemed fit for faculty housing. You read Beckett and I read Kierkegaard and I rested my head on your rib cage and after hours of reading interspersed with nodding off we went inside and ate leftovers and held each other through the night.

I haven't spent a day with you since when I haven't thought, *This feels right.*

Which is not to say that we haven't had hard days. Days when I preferred not to speak to you.

Isn't it awkward to date someone you met while standing naked in front of a room full of strangers? Sometimes people ask us this. But the answer is no. Quite the opposite.

I wasn't sure I'd go through with it when I saw the art modeling guild's audition flyer, but the money was decent, the head space for writing was attractive, and the rules set by the guild were clear. Breaks from posing every twenty minutes. Room always heated to the model's comfort. And artists never allowed to harass or touch us. There were rules for the models to follow, too, of course — some of them unspoken, rules I came to love.

You must always do your best for the artists. You must reveal not just your body but your naked self, within the world you and the artists create together. In this way, enforced distance allows for a different kind of closeness.

Could we make that kind of world together, outside the studio? The night you came back to my apartment, you stripped off your clothes as fast as I did. Stood naked before me, your body lean but not brute. A collaboration, this world, where we could have it all. Distance and closeness. The beauty of paradox.

But our world of two seemed to be cracking in those days just before we found the foster agency.

We had moved back from North Carolina to San Francisco. The honeymoon over. In North Carolina, for the sake of health insurance, I'd taught and raced from class to class to department meeting to office hours. You'd painted, in the rented studio my wages supported. You were downtrodden about the kind of painting you were doing and how it wasn't the kind of thing anyone would buy, but I loved it. I was happy, with you painting in your studio and cooking us dinner and me working. Then we came back to California. Then there was no studio. Then *you* were the one racing from class to class to department meeting; and I worked, too, and bought us takeout.

You said I was living like a single person. That I didn't care enough about having a real dinner together every night. You noted that I bought my own carton of skim milk. Said we should compromise and drink 2 percent. You said, "A family should drink the same milk."

Unspoken rules I'd not been aware of.

We almost went to counseling over milk.

Then we found the foster agency. Then we had a common mission. Maybe two cartons of milk were okay, you said, since we were in this together. The fights stopped.

Would we fight like that again if it doesn't work out with . . . ? But I can't even think her name.

The nights Maresa spends at Auntie's, the recurring dream comes to me again. The dream I had even through the worst of the milk-fight days. In the dream, I am being forced to marry my ex-husband Max, and I'm thinking *this feels wrong this feels wrong this feels wrong*. Then I realize: *Wait. I'm married to Sebastian*. And I wake up thinking *thank God thank God thank God thank God*.

At nightfall on the third day, we go out into the garage, where I've unrolled a carpet, set up your easel.

We used to have sessions like this every few weeks, sessions when I gave you twisty, decidedly nonclassical poses, sessions when you drew for two hours and then began your own strip, joined me naked on the carpet. Sessions like the time when you made the pastel portrait that used to hang next to our bed, beside your wooden crucifix. The portrait with my messy hair, my breasts, my face. The breasts small yet pendulous, the nipples wide and soft. I don't like my breasts much. I didn't think the portrait was flattering. But it was true. I asked you, immediately, to frame it. It was who I was. It was who you were.

⌒

When we were getting the house ready for the foster home certification, I took the portrait down. Bare breasts and all that.
Shouldn't we leave it up? you said. This is who we are, you said,
they should know that. But when the far-off county worker
came with the binder, you removed it.

Maybe someday we can hang it again, you said.

But it doesn't feel like us anymore. You can't just put things
back in their old places.

On the fourth day of the quiet, the last day, my blessedly blunt
best friend comes to visit. She admires the tomato plants. "So
peaceful," she says. Months ago, when I first showed her Maresa's photo, she choked up, dabbed her eyes like the mother of
the bride. Now I show her the photos Auntie texts us from the
fireworks show. Maresa and her former foster sisters, sparks
flying from lit sticks in their hands.
    We sit beneath the birch tree drinking Pinot Gris. My friend
knows everything that's happened with the girl we call daughter. She asks if we feel ready for more.
    The answer is no.
    She doesn't ask again about regrets.

Ten

We missed you!" we tell her.

We are not exactly being sincere. Which is not to say we aren't grieved by the idea of separation, past or future.

"We don't feel we need the whole team," we tell the grey-crowned worker. "We were hoping to meet just with you."

Now that Maresa's back from Auntie's, so is the entourage.

"We need to be proactive," the grey-crowned worker says. "When people start setting deadlines, the placement isn't going well."

We didn't say it was a deadline, did we, my love? You just said you didn't want to think about finalizing, for a while. And I said maybe we should take three months for observing. Not that we would tell Maresa any of this; she wouldn't have to know. Just give us all some space. Then reassess.

Ah, "assessing," that's the buzzword.

"We want you to know that no one here is judging you," announces the new agency supervisor at the head of the conference table. She is slim and of reassuring height, with hair like an exuberant mushroom. In the other faux-leather chairs: me, you, the grey-crowned social worker, the bimple therapist, the brunette Family Support Specialist. I am wearing yoga pants covered in cat hair because I haven't managed to get the laundry done. The bimple therapist is wearing a jade-green silk shirt-dress and snakeskin heels. The Family Support Specialist is wearing a sheer lace blouse over a camisole and pleated pants. "Well, I guess I just told you we think you're doing a good job," the supervisor says, adding a nose-crinkling smile. "So, okay, in some ways we *are* judging you. But not really judging, right? Assessing."

We've been assessing, too. Comparing evidence, one could say. Maresa had a therapist back when she lived with Auntie. We had a phone call with that therapist the week before Maresa's move. We learned that Maresa talked with this therapist about many things: her birth mom, her sister, why she pulled Auntie's hair. One time she told the therapist, "I pulled Auntie's hair because I wanted to test if she loved me."

"She's remarkably self-aware and emotionally articulate for seven years old," this therapist told us. Which squared with our impression.

Five months of sessions now with the blonde bimple therapist. Sometimes Maresa does her therapy appointments alone, and walks back out into the reception area of the cinderblock building munching bean chips and slurping fruit punch and carrying tiny plastic toys, all given to her by the bimple therapist. Sometimes I go to Maresa's therapy appointments with her, fifty minutes of sinking our hands in the sandbox and popping our fingers up like little puppets that say "Hi, who are you?" and the therapist's little finger bending and saying, "How are you feeling, Maresa?" and Maresa making a sound like an angry cat and then baby Maresa's voice saying, "Can I have some bean chips?" And then bimple therapist goes off to fetch the snacks.

Often, Daddy, you and I meet with the therapist in lieu of Maresa doing a session, since the therapist has emphasized that this kind of therapy is as much about training the parents as it is about working with the child.

And twice, Daddy, you've gone with Maresa to her appointments. Done the digging-around-in-the-sand thing. Brought Maresa home with chips and a bottle of fruit punch. Asked me, "Does it seem to you like . . . anything's actually happening there?"

Now I turn my face from the supervisor, look across the conference table at the blonde therapist. "Yes, we'll start going to the support groups." And yes, we'll check in monthly with the new parent mentor; yes, we'll read the pile of parenting books they gave us; yes, we'll go to the weekend prerequisite training for finalizing even though we're not ready; yes, yes, we'll do whatever you prescribe. I'm too tired for any other words. So you're the one, my love, who ventures the question we've agreed to bring up.

"Since we're all gathered," you say, "we'd like to check in on how Maresa's therapy is going."

"Oh." The therapist's face contracting like we just poked her with a stick, dangly earrings swaying. "Well. How do *you* think it's going?"

Oh Sebastian, my lamb, that squirm-inducing flat affect of

yours. How I love it in this moment. "We really don't know. That's why we're asking for your professional opinion."

The bimple therapist and the Family Support Specialist making eye contact.

I saw them out on the town a couple of Fridays ago. I was taking Maresa for ice cream, and they were striding on their heels and laughing, arm in arm. Spotting Maresa and saying, "Hey! Hi there, sweetie," and striding on with their blow-dried hair swaying.

I know it shouldn't have bothered me to see that.

The therapist looks up at me with her Concerned face. "I think the sand play process is starting to unearth some of Maresa's anxieties about family," she says, then adds, "It's slow progress right now, though, because Maresa is, unfortunately, not particularly self-aware or, well, emotionally articulate."

The therapist and the Family Support Specialist watching you and me make eye contact.

The supervisor with the exuberant mushroom hair is very good at uplift. "Well, this has been an open and productive meeting, I think," she says with a hair-bounce worthy of a shampoo commercial, "and the *main* thing we here at the agency want to communicate is that we're here for you. We so admire the work you're doing and we can see that you're committed, so . . . we're here for you!" Guiding us, like a game-show model, to the door.

There's another family waiting in the lobby. We know this family because the little girl, Lilly, was in Maresa's first-grade class. Lilly is not being adopted. Lilly is here with her birth mom and her birth mom's boyfriend, who is holding twin babies and shouting at Lilly's ten-year-old brother, Nathaniel, "Knock it off, jackass!" You wouldn't think he'd say that here in the agency building, but I can't claim to be shocked, because it's the kind of thing I hear the boyfriend say to Lilly when I'm picking Maresa up from school.

It took me a while to figure out that this agency serves two populations. One: people adopting children out of foster care. Two: birth parents trying to keep their children *out* of foster care — that is, parents court-ordered to go to "family preservation services."

I may have the numbering backward.

Lilly's mom and the mom's boyfriend are living with Lilly and her siblings in a hotel. You and I know this, Daddy, because a couple of months ago we served them dinner at the homeless feeding sponsored by our church.

"I don't think that's such a good thing to do with Maresa after all," you said when we got home. We'd both noticed the trembling of Maresa's lips when we'd finished cleaning up the church kitchen. "Lilly's family yells at her," she said.

I don't want to judge Lilly's family. I want to tell myself I'm "assessing." The mother's boyfriend covered in tattoos. I've gotten a good look at him, since he and Lilly's family always seem to be walking out of the cinderblock building just as Maresa and I are walking in. His missing teeth.

I have to get her out of here I have to get her out of here I have to get her out of here.

⌒

"Sorry about the, uh, colorful language," the mom's boyfriend is calling out to the bimple therapist and the Family Support Specialist as we cross the lobby. Lilly's mother smiling at me, but I never know how to make eye contact with her. Lilly opening a bag of bean chips.

"Jack's still working on his filthy mouth," Lilly's mom says with a roll of the eyes.

I watch bimple therapist give Lilly's mom her Loving face. The face that, when trained on me, makes me feel like a pitiable and despicable person.

"Well, we're all doing our best," she says to Lilly's mom and the man with missing teeth.

We admire the work you're doing. We can see that you're committed and we're here for you!

Thank God Maresa hasn't come with us this time. Thank God we don't have to walk her, yet again, past Lilly's mom and the cussing boyfriend.

You take the driver's side, start the engine. "We have to stop taking Maresa here," you say.

Eleven

BUT FIRST WE WANT an evaluation from the county psychiatrist, and bimple therapist is our ticket. The "referring clinician."

So: another cinderblock building, on the other side of town. We sit on kid-sized chairs in the play area and take cues in an elaborate waiting game. First just bimple therapist goes in, then bimple therapist and Maresa, then us, then Maresa is sent again to the playroom while bimple therapist watches you and me talking with the doctor. Watches us and takes notes.

"Maresa is remarkably articulate and has impressive inner resources," the psychiatrist says. His plaid shirt is cuffed and ironed, but the top button is open — a PhD version of surfer dude. *Severe PTSD*, he has written on his pad.

"The problem with psychotropic medications and children," the doctor says, "is that when the child is numbed out, she's not processing the real issues."

Bimple therapist nods and speaks before we do. "Yes, we feel that Maresa —"

Which is when I blurt, "Who is *we?*"

Interesting, the doctor's face says, not without kindness. Letting the question hang as bimple therapist tucks a lock of hair behind her ears and we all try to pretend I didn't say that. "How about we'll hold off on medicating for now," the psychiatrist finally says. "But we'll keep the case open, so if you ever need another appointment" — looking at me and you, Sebastian, not at the therapist — "you just call."

The next day, we make the implications of what I'd blurted official. "We've decided we need a different therapist," I tell the grey-crowned social worker.

Silence on the line. "I wonder if your expectations of therapy have been realistic," she finally says. And informs me that we'll lose the services of the Family Support Specialist. Evidently she and the bimple therapist were a package deal.

Bimple therapist says she needs to schedule at least one more session. For closure. "We should minimize the shock Maresa will experience," she says. "She's already lost so many people she's been asked to trust."

So we take Maresa for that session. And the day after, the bimple therapist calls. "I sensed at our last session that Maresa was apprehensive about ending. If you're willing . . . we really should do one more."

The day I'm scheduled to take Maresa in for *that* final session, the therapist calls you, Sebastian, to see about scheduling another session for the following week. You're in San Francisco teaching your summer courses, but you call me after class to report your verbatim response. "I've discussed this thoroughly with my wife," you told the therapist, "and this week's session will be Maresa's last."

Ten minutes later, my phone rings again. "Hi, how are you? I know you're bringing Maresa for her session after school, but I thought I'd go ahead and check with you about scheduling next week's appointment."

I'm alone in my writing office but I feel her giving me the Look of Professionalism. "But I thought my husband . . . Didn't you just call him?"

"Oh. We must have had a misunderstanding."

"Well, everything's clear now. Yes?"

Today's outfit: black shirtdress, suede heels. "Maresa, before we get started, I need to talk with your mommy for just a bit, okay?" Settling Maresa into the cinderblock waiting room and pushing a video into the VCR. Leading me down the hallway, that discreet kneeling motion to flick on the white-noise machine as the door closes.

"Now, I know your husband feels —"

Say as little as possible, that was good advice, my love. But I'm congenitally incapable of following it.

"I don't like the way you've treated us," I start.

I say I feel she's never really listened to us. I say I've felt coerced. Disempowered, when I'm trying to be Maresa's parent. Does the therapist stare at me for two minutes, five? "I can see you feel strongly," she says. "Is there anything else?" But I can no longer speak.

So we walk back out to the waiting room in silence. "Hi, sweetie!" bimple therapist says to Maresa, and they head off down the hall. While I sit staring at a stack of *People* magazines. Forty minutes ticking down, a long time to hide one's shaking hands from the receptionist.

Then down the hall comes Maresa, carrying fruit punch and bean chips in one hand, a large shopping bag in the other. "Look what Lisa gave me!" Four skeins of yarn, a paint set, coloring books. A wooden box that comes with tiny plastic jewels to affix with glue.

"Why did she give me so many presents, Mommy?"

I'm driving Maresa home, but I'm still thinking of the therapist's eyes as we stood at the threshold. How she nearly cried. Pain of a woman who wants to save.

Protector rendered powerless.

Twelve

Before i married him, between our blowout fights, my ex-husband Max used to put me "on probation." Every time he packed up and left, he moved a couple of blocks farther away. But when I called at midnight, he'd summon a taxi and be at my door within the hour. Mornings after those reunions, we'd eat brunch at the corner greasy spoon, spread out the *New York Times* like always. I'd watch him watch me, as if I were a ticking bomb. Shaking as he poured the maple syrup.

Your visit apparently wore down even Auntie's sentimentalism, Little One. You refused to eat her cooking. Hit the other girls with your glow-in-the-dark stick at the fireworks show. She doesn't ask, in her texts, about "next time."
    — *I forgot how difficult she is! Hope you find the right therapist soon. God be with you!*

Daddy's been thinking aloud about Brenda and Joe. The decertified couple. We glimpse their names again in your medical records, taking you for a checkup. One night, you and Daddy are playing checkers at the pizza parlor when you say, "Joe shouted a lot and he scared me, but he was really good at checkers."

You and your sister lived with Brenda and Joe for a year. Brenda and Joe loved nature. They took you to the ocean. Took you camping.

"They really did try," Daddy says to me, late, as the crickets crescendo outside the bedroom window. Your medical history binder open on his lap, as though the trail of doctors' visits to treat your split chin, your broken finger, your broken arm, might lead to some conclusion.

"God, they must be heartbroken. God, they tried their hardest."

I've been taking out the letters from Susannah. We've had no communication from Brenda and Joe, but we hear from Susannah every few months. She sends old photos, this sweet-smiled woman with brown braided hair and thick glasses, and there you are behind her, helmeted, in the saddle. She sends presents — a model horse that looks just like the palomino you used to ride at her equine therapy ranch. You never play with the toy horse, though you do tell us you had to shovel horse poop every morning. I can't figure out how long you lived with Susannah. One month? Two? Susannah was young and single, the social workers from the far-off county explained. She was calling them daily, they said, asking them to help you get dressed for school. Asking them to help you stop screaming.

In one letter to you, Little One, she writes about the key. It hangs on a necklace, and it's stamped with the word LOVED.

Whenever you're feeling sad, Maresa, you just hold your key and know that you are always in my heart.

You wore the necklace to school one day, Little One, and lost it on the playground. Cried for two hours. We called Susannah to see how we could get you an exact replacement. Turned out she'd bought the necklace from a trendy online outfit. Fifty bucks. "Ouch," Daddy said. He'd just learned the community college was cutting one class from his adjunct load in the fall. "We can't afford to be buying fifty-dollar necklaces."

But we had to, I said; so we ordered it. The day after it arrived, you wore the shiny new key to school, the word LOVED glinting. When I picked you up that afternoon, you were crying. It was gone.

In her first letter to us, Susannah revealed that she'd been a foster child, too.

That's how I know she can make it through, with enough love. She's tough, but she's worth it! Stick with her, don't give up!

I snorted at those words when I first read them. *Stick with her,* says the woman who didn't. Then, I heard unearned patronizing. Now I hear guilt. Now I read these letters again in the garden at sunset, and crickets are the only sound.

Thirteen

ALL FURTHER SUMMER family travels: canceled. I can't say this sacrifice pains me. Five days in a lakeside cabin with my brother and his wife and your cousins: no longer so attractive.

I do travel alone, though. Make a few getaways to my best friend's. Drive down to give a reading in San Francisco, and once to see a performance of *Tosca*. In the ring of the soprano's middle register I hear your "opera voice." I hear you in the arias and my eyes sting. "There must be a story behind that red heart you're wearing!" says a woman at intermission, pointing to the clay pendant you shaped the week you moved in, and I excuse myself to the bathroom, tissue off the rivulet of mascara, pull myself together, and browse the gift shop. Forget to bring back presents.

Daddy's the one who brings you gifts from his sojourns. Every time. A color wheel to aid your acrylics experimenting after he returns from a Matisse exhibition. A picture book of dogs holding yoga poses when he's back from the used-book fair. A golden retriever doing Warrior III, you could laugh at that all

night. While I watch your face in profile, the dimple disappearing and reappearing and disappearing again.

And the boom box. That's Daddy's idea. "She needs her own
music," he says, researching Japanese brands on the internet at
midnight.

Auntie taught you never to say "Oh my God," but still that's
what you shout when you see it, the stereo. Then blast the
Christian rock station.

Thanks be to God for the YMCA. Up at 7:45, at camp by 8:30,
day after day. Lanyard-making, thanks be to God for lanyards.
You twist together miles of plastic ribbons — you're a one-kid
woven-plastic keychain factory.

Not everyone in the online memoir class this quarter is a re-
tiree. There are middle-aged mothers, too: one who is raising
an autistic child, one whose son has a proprioceptive disorder that causes him to scream half the day. Of all my students,
these women have the least time for writing, but consistently
their pages are the most astonishing, their honesty the most
arresting. They are stuck with these children. They love these
children. The retirees admire their pages. The critiques they
post in the workshop discussion threads mention *wisdom* and
grace.

I read their pages in my office overlooking the garden while,
in a park clubhouse two miles away, you weave lanyards. While,
in the garage, Daddy unpacks paintings he made decades ago,
paintings he tells me are junk.

We eat dinners outside, drenched in mosquito repellent. A fox
pokes his head from behind the garage. We never see the deer;

she comes after nightfall, munches the fruit on the nectarine tree, deposits piles of dung pellets shiny as bullets.

"Guess we'd better build that fence," Daddy says. "And we'll need a gate if we're actually going to get you a dog." We've called the shelters and they're firm on the rules, to the point of inspecting the property. I should have known they'd be strict about this, all those months I spent dog-walking, back in my former life.

One of the retirees is torn between topics. She could write about her year of cooking in Sicily. But what she really wants to write about, she confesses during a video meeting with the graceful, wise mothers, is the year she and her husband spent trying to adopt her grandson.

The grandson's mother was living in a hotel with the boy and doing heroin when protective services stepped in. "We wanted to help him — we did our best — but people don't realize, it's not so simple to help a kid like that." This videoconferencing stuff is awkward; each participant's face stares back at her as we stare at the one speaking, watch her brow crumple. She mentions failure. She mentions devastation.

Write about it, the other students urge. Get it on paper!

"I just don't know if I can. Even though it was ten years ago, every time I think of Dylan — I just start crying."

"You know, I've always wanted to read about Sicilian cuisine," I say.

Whyyyyyyyyyyyy MCA! Little daily disco hymn. I teach you the moves. Every night before brushing our teeth we play the song on your boom box and boogie into alphabet shapes.

⌒

You're hitting other kids more. You have a tendency to whack them in the face with a lanyard or Wiffle ball bat at the YMCA camp. When we move on to science camp, though, you're all business. Thirteen little boys, one other girl, and you. Who knew this camp would be your favorite? Every day you fixate for hours on touching a nail with a wire to ignite a bulb, or pouring vinegar into baking soda. Then I pick you up and we cross the street to the town pool. There's a snack shack where I buy you Creamsicles. A teenage lifeguard every six feet.

You pass the underwater swimming test and win entry to the deep end, littlest kid I see there. Touching bottom, racing up. Touching bottom, racing up. Pretty lonely in that deep end. By the fourth day you've joined the other kids for Marco Polo. You seem to get along best with the slightly older girls. You're strong and they like that. You don't hit them or splash them in the face. You laugh with them. You play. Then one day I see you teaching a boy littler than you to do underwater handstands.

I sit on the bench, sucking an Otter Pop. Laptop sliding on sweaty thighs. Looking at you, glistening like a mermaid, then back at the screen. You again, the screen. My final workshop letters are more glowing than usual this quarter. *Thank you for trusting me with your life story*, I write to my summer students. *What a privilege it has been to witness your growth.*

Every Sunday we go to church. Then to the coffee shop, where you always get steamed milk with vanilla and whipped cream on top and you read the Sunday funnies with Daddy. Then we go home and work in the garden together, or more accurately, Daddy and I work in the garden while you dig moats in the sand pile. Then to Grandma Elsie and Grandpa Bob's for dinner.

"Am I crazy or is this getting easier?"

"Shhh!" Daddy says. "Don't jinx it."

You have a new thing for conspiracies, two against one. Like when it's my birthday and you get Daddy to take you to the florist down the street to assemble a bouquet that includes one red rose, two stems of snapdragons, a pink carnation, and one daffodil. You hide it in the garage, rub your palms like a super-villain: "Daddy and I have a *seeeeeecret!*"

The day we hide my six-pack of Diet Cokes in the garage, Little One, you're bubbling over like one of your science experiments. "I won't tell Daddy, I won't!"

Daddy doesn't approve of diet sodas and he won't abide Mc-Donald's.

"Pleeeeease?" you say as we pass the golden arches.

"Okay," I say. "Our secret."

"We have a secret!" you say, as I pass the fudge McSundae to the back seat.

Daddy has noticed the new bumper sticker trend. We're driving home on the freeway from his birthday dinner at Grandma Elsie and Grandpa Bob's when he points it out. "What is up with those?" he says. ANTHONY. 1982–2012. IN LOVING MEMORY, reads the decal on the Suburban in front of us. It's true, I've been seeing them on half the trucks and SUVs in this town.

"Whatever you do when I die," Daddy says, "please don't make me a bumper sticker, all right?"

I wink at you in the rearview mirror, Little One, and the in-dents on your cheeks wink back. "Oh, come on, Daddy," I say. "I thought we'd slap it right next to the honor student sticker.

SEBASTIAN GRUBER, IN LOVING MEMORY. With maybe, you know, a drawing of that little boy peeing!"

"*Mommy!*"

You're in a fit of laughter, Little One. Beautiful laughter.

"A little boy peeing right on your name, Daddy, wouldn't you like that?" I'm on a roll. "Your name in great big letters on the back of the car, REST IN PEACE."

"Mommy!"

We crack up the whole drive home, and by the time Daddy unlocks the door and you push inside and run to your bedroom, you're laughing and shouting, "I have to write this down!"

You still write your b's and d's backward. It's one of life's daily pleasures, along with the way you describe the morning meal as "breaf-kast."

Daddy and the bumpr stickr when he bies, reads the ripped page you wave at us.

I take a picture of this page with my phone. I have an urge to post it on Facebook.

Eight kinds: Cherokee Purple, Brandywine, San Marzano, Cherry, Beefsteak, Mortgage Lifter, Hillbilly, Green Zebra. Maybe a week more and they'll be ripe. What will we do with them all?

"You'll have to eat them all, Mommy. You'll get gigantic fat!"

We eat corn dogs and cotton candy at the county fair. You ride the Tilt-a-Whirl, the Rocket Blast. Won't smile on the rides, too miffed that your height limits you to the "baby stuff."

"That wasn't *really* fun," you say as we drive home. But the photo I took of you and Daddy chomping corn dogs — could've fooled me. New screen saver for my phone.

⌒

I harvest a handful of tomatoes early, can't resist. The next morning the garden is strewn. Ripe tomatoes tossed everywhere like the detritus of a frat party. Each one missing a chomp the size of a deer's mouth. I pick them up and pitch them in the compost pile.

"Somehow it's the ingratitude that's the worst, isn't it?" Daddy laughs.

Half-successful thought experiment: I am happy the deer got what she needed.

"Your color is looking good, my love. You seem so healthy lately."

"Shhhh!" Daddy says. "Don't jinx it."

As a family, we don't like the candidate whose name rhymes with "dump." The man Auntie told you was going to make the whole country rich when she drove you around in her red Durango on the Fourth of July.

You hear him on the radio, talking about a wall and bad *hombres*. You hear snippets of the debates because Daddy and I can't stand not to listen.

"'Oh, I'm a *gentleman*,'" you say in droll imitation.

"He's a big fat drunk dump!" you announce over dinner.

We don't make fun of people for their weight, we say.

"Stupid drunk dump?"

Fair enough.

There are Post-it notes over the two sides of the sink. DIRTY. CLEAN. Daddy looks over his shoulder, catches my eye.

He went over the protocol with me again last week, because

I'd broken another bowl. It's a universal system, he said, in the kind of voice used for disciplining a dog. Basic sanitation. "We keep all the dirty on one side, all the clean on the other, and the clean side must always be kept absolutely clean. You got that now?"

He's up late answering "reply all" department emails and writing his Annual Reflection and Self-Examination. *Please provide concrete examples of both your pedagogical and research/creative achievements this past academic year,* the prompt reads. "Oh, God, leave off that awful admin crap," I say. "Go out to the garage and draw for a while." When he gives me the evil eye I remember: I left my oatmeal pan on the CLEAN side this morning.

"You don't have to be so stern about it," I say when I overhear him chiding you about leaving your dirty clothes on the floor. Thinking of his voice when he gave me last night's tutorial on proper cutting-board maintenance, how the board must be laid to dry at a precise angle of aeration upon certain cutting-board-appropriate dishtowels.

"Is it possible you're overthinking this?" I'd asked.

"I wish you valued me," he said.

Ah, a word with an echo. Over the summer, the adjuncts at Daddy's college decided, once again, to agitate for a raise. Tired of ignoring the indignity. They made charts like the one that circulated on Facebook, McDonald's instructing its workers how to live on the edge of the poverty line. The adjuncts broke it all down, the effective hourly pay of teaching a ten-week course for less than four thousand dollars.

"What did she say?" I asked Daddy after the big meeting with the VP of academic affairs.

"That she wished they could do more, but this was the fiscal reality of American higher education."

"That's it?"

"Oh, and: We greatly value your contributions."

His fall quarter's about to start, which means soon, once again, he'll be gone three days a week.

I'm looking ahead to fall, too. Planning to change up the syllabus for my memoir class. Try out some readings with unusual points of view. I'm drawn to this certain short essay written by a woman who, as a kid, saw something shocking. She lived out in the desert, and one day, as a monsoon began and the arroyo rushed, she and all the neighborhood kids saw a boy jump onto a plank of wood like a surfboard, watched him ride the torrent and smash into a bridge. The thing I find fascinating about the essay: There's not a single "I." The entire thing is written from the perspective of "we." A "we" that can see the whole scene, hold everyone in it.

"How did she do that?" the retirees ask during our last session of the summer, when I tell them what I'm chewing on.

"That's what I'd like to figure out," I say.

Fourteen

Y<small>OU,</small> <small>SEBASTIAN</small>. And you, Little One.

I want to be connected to both of you, at the same time. I believed three was a magic number, and all that *Schoolhouse Rock!* jive.

Why is the geometry not working?

"How did you two meet?" the potential new therapist with the office on Main Street asks, and I tell her about how I was the model sent to his art class, how I could see he was so kind and patient with his students. "Ooh, two bohemians," she says. "How romantic. Important to have that solid connection if you're going to do this kind of parenting."

We spend twenty minutes signing consent forms, including "the standard stuff" on client confidentiality. "Small town!" the therapist says, her skin stretched like cellophane. You distrust people with plastic surgery, I know. She asks whether Maresa has difficulties trusting men, and we tell her about the times she's snapped into a dissociative state and thought you were choking her.

"Oh, the Dillards' boy is like that, too. God, he's put that father through the wringer! So tough with sexual abuse in the background. You know the Dillards, right? I think they worked with your same agency."

Only I catch your arched eyebrow. "Small town!" you say, and nod at the confidentiality form.

Crossing another name off the list of therapists recommended by the agency supervisor.

"I know we can't stretch this out," you say. "But we want to get this right."

Sometimes at midnight, Little One, when you're chasing me through the house like a sleepless gremlin, I wish we'd gone ahead and gotten you those meds. Sometimes I'd be happy to disavow my former high-minded principles. I declined psycho-tropic drugs when I went through my breakdown in college, in my period of leaving steak knives in boxes. Not because I re-fused to admit I had problems. Because I wanted to face them.

But I was twenty-one, Little One. You're seven.

"It seems like she wants to trust you but hasn't quite attached to you as what we in the profession call 'the good object.'" So said the psychiatrist. Looking at me.

Would attaching to me as "the good object" make your birth mother "the bad object"?

Your birth father is the unknown object. Just a name. We show you the birth certificate as we work on your life book. We've made a whole page about how you were born at 1:33 p.m. in Tuscaloosa, Alabama.

"Tuscaloosa, Tuscaloosa, Tuscaloosa, Tuscaloosa!" you chant while skipping around the house. We're reading *Alice in Wonderland* at bedtime, but I don't think you're consciously trying to impersonate the Mad Hatter.

We write a page about your birth mother. You draw a picture of her from a photograph. You say your drawing is terrible, but I'm impressed. She's holding up a cell phone, taking a selfie. You've captured a twinkle of conspiracy in your mother's eye that strikes me as true.

Another day. Another page in the life book. *My birth daddy's name is Juan Chavez*, you write. *I never met him. I love Juan Chavez.*

"Write the rest for me," you say, and give me the pencil. I don't question what you dictate. *I remember he set a blanket down on the counter. And he set me down. On the counter. His arms were soft. He changed my diaper. I cried because my diaper was smelly.*

Soon when I get a car I'm going to find him in Mexico or Tuscaloosa.

Another portrait. You're very good at noses now, and his resembles yours, a bit broad, well-spaced nostrils. The eyes are detailed. You spend a long time on the shading, working to rub the charcoal just as Daddy taught you. "I think that would be his skin color, kind of dark but not really really dark," you tell me. I say I think you nailed it. It's exactly like your beautiful skin, I say.

The next day, after the pool, I've killed the engine and you're sitting very still in the back seat.

"Why can't I meet my daddy?"

"Well, nobody knows where he is, sweetheart. I'm so sorry. Someday, when the time is right, we'll help you find him."

"I didn't get to know my daddy." Fists balled. "I *want* my daddy." Seat belt still buckled. "I WANT MY *DADDY!*"

I reach to the back seat. You scream. But you let me rub your shin while you cry.

My daddy was a fantasy, too. The man who took me to the pizza parlor on Saturdays. Who danced with my feet on his feet to New Wave rock every other Sunday morning. When he showed up at the train station with alcohol on his breath, the fantasy started to crack. And then came the night of the blood.

In the ER that night, 4:30 a.m., I sat on my grandmother's lap. The doctor looked down and asked my grandmother if she wanted to see the body.

After he died, a recurring dream: My father had actually lived. He just didn't want to see me.

In the absence of your birth father, you were left with your mother's boyfriends. Sometimes when you tell me you don't like men who shout and cuss, I say I understand. I tell you that my mother, your Grandma Annie, married one of her boyfriends back when I was a little girl, way before she met Papa Tim. She married him because my little brother, son of this boyfriend, was growing inside her belly. I say I lived with this man for seven years, and he hated me, and he shouted the F-word at me, like your mom's boyfriends did at you.

Ah, a mother's boyfriends. One of my earliest memories of my stepfather: He caught a rat in a spring trap, then gouged the eyes out with a screwdriver. Laughing.

And one time: He burned me with a cigarette on purpose.

"No kid should have to go through anything like that," I tell you. "But I'm okay now. The more I faced it, the less I was afraid. That's how I know that whatever happened, you can face it, too."

You are neither moved nor impressed. "You still had your mom," you say.

You say your mother's boyfriends hated the way you woke them up in the morning. My mother's boyfriend hated the way I did the dishes. I didn't like to soak them in dirty water, didn't like to plunge my hands in the murk. My stepfather would stand behind me. Twice my girth. Ready to grab a dish from my hands and smash it.

And here I stand again at the sink three decades later, washing dishes on an August night. Of course, Sebastian, you would never smash a dish. No. But you have been sulking. Over what you think your wife and daughter should eat, and over housekeeping.

"It's not sanitary to let the dishwater sit overnight," you say now with a warning glance.

I scour the iron skillet. *Soon he'll be telling me I can't buy my own milk.*

Grandma Annie says you're easy to live with otherwise, let that stuff go.

You make the bed in a different manner than I was taught. The top sheet, you say, must be put on with the patterned side facing down, so that when the edge of the top sheet is turned over the quilt (exactly three inches showing), the sheet pattern will be properly displayed.

What the Family Support Specialist said when we told her about Maresa making the bed: "Your expectations *might* be a bit high for age seven."

In my imagination, as I wash the dishes, I return to my old studio apartment. Walking in alone after a day of art modeling — what bliss. *Click, click, click.* The moon shining through the far window. The dishes stacked clean in the rack. The bed made the way I like it. No one scrutinizing.

Your most stinging complaint is back, justification for the Post-it notes above the sink. "Since you want to live like roommates, I'll *treat* you like one."

"You're too hard on me!" I say. And then we hear the creak of the bedroom door, and there is the Little One.

"Be nice to Mommy."

"All right now," you say softly. "Go back to bed."

"We can't fight in front of her," you say, and I know you're right. "We don't want her taking sides."

Oh, but that's the problem in my dark impulsive heart: Sometimes I do.

The next day when we leave for church, the fuel light is flashing. "I've asked you not to let the gas get that low," you say, and though I see her gaze in the rearview mirror, I don't stop myself.

"Can't you lay off? Why are you so hard on me?"

Summer's down to its last few days. Surfer dude is sitting in a patio chair. His first visit since the waterslide park.

Maresa sits cross-legged next to the house, smashing rocks against weeds, an occupation she calls "making wheat." She's wearing a too-small, two-year-old tap-dance recital costume, red sequined shorts attached to a black-and-white-checkered top. There's a bow tie that's supposed to snap closed at the neck, only she's got the costume on backward.

"So, Maresa, uh, how's it going?" surfer dude asks.

"Great!" she says, teeth gritted as she smashes. Then Daddy comes out with four glasses of lemonade on a tray.

"I want her to be my mommy," she says suddenly, pointing at me. "But I don't want *him* to be my daddy."

I stand in the middle. Caught.

"Maresa!" I say. But there's so much I can't say to you.

Our third date. His ashen skin, his thinness. Over pizza and beer, he told me the words. *Atrial septal.* And that night, for the first time, he came back to my apartment.

Plenty of men, in those years after Max, had come back to my apartment. And always, if they were still there in the morning, I was seized by a sudden horror that I'd made a terrible mistake.

I was seized by this same horror that first morning with the man I now think of as Daddy.

But then, as he slept, I watched his heart. Counted the beats. Took my laptop into the bathroom and fumbled to remember the term he'd spoken over dinner.

Several patients tolerate large unrepaired defects for 80 years or even longer without serious disability. However, it is assumed that, as a rule, atrial septal defect reduces life expectancy, the average age at death not exceeding 50 years.

Don't worry, Little One — the doctor says that with his surgery, Daddy's life expectancy is not actually *that* bad, and most
days we believe the doctor. But I didn't know what Daddy's
doctor had said that morning when I searched "atrial septal." I
didn't know if he had two years or twenty. I only felt all horror
leave my body. I only felt my own heart speed.

Here's something I can't say to you, Little One, because I'm not
sure you'd understand. It's easy to take the wrong way. Reason
#1 I married Daddy: I knew he was going to die. I mean, viscer-
ally understood this. Which meant he was a real person. Not
an abstraction in my imagination like all the other men, men I
feared would either leave, like my fantasy father, or stay and become . . . flawed. Less than perfect for me, in some impossible-
to-predict way. I can't explain how this hit me, how — for the
first time — I got it. This weird, kind man wouldn't be here forever. He was a real person, simultaneously precious and imper-
fect. Like me.
       Which meant my own selfish fears were finally moot.

And I don't know where this factor ranks, but I do know it's
a reason for trying to adopt you: I hoped you'd remember
Daddy fondly with me, when the awful time came, when you
were grown. I thought missing him together would be a buffer
against grief.

"How about we go for a walk?" surfer dude finally says. "Just me
and you, Maresa."
       I watch you head off, holding Daddy's hand in the garden.
"I'm sorry, my love," I tell him. Not quite knowing for whom
I'm apologizing.

⌒

When you and surfer dude come back, you grind weeds again, as the grownups watch from across the yard.

"Hard to know what's going on with the daddy stuff," surfer dude says. "This probably sounds crazy, but — try not to take what she says to heart. She told me she likes it here. I asked if she wanted to change anything, and she said, 'Just my attitude.'"

But I don't want you to change your attitude, Little One. I want you to change your heart.

"It's a triangle," I tell you that night. "The three of us have to be equally connected, see? No two against one, Maresa honey. That's the only way it works."

I think of our hardest day, Little One, back in February. The afternoon you brought home the drawing of the warty, snaggletoothed woman. I asked you who it was. You looked me in the eye: "You." Daddy was grading his students' museum reports that afternoon. I had to get you out of the house so that Daddy could work. This task seemed impossible. Your drawing left me speechless. I took you on a walk through the pines. I could not even look at you.

And then the next day, it was like you'd had amnesia. "You're the best mommy!"

And suddenly I had amnesia, too.

The day after your walk with surfer dude, Daddy is hoisting you on his shoulder and calling out, "Sack of potatoes! Hey, where can I put this sack of potatoes!"

"Mommy!" you shout. "You're nice, but Daddy's way more fun!"

Say it, I pray. *Please say it.*
"You're the best daddy!"

Another of his good qualities: He doesn't hold a grudge. Not a week after you told him you didn't want him to be your daddy, this strange man I married rolls out butcher paper. Spills a bucket of markers across the floor. "What should it say?" he asks, and you shrug.

"How about SECOND GRADE ROCKS!" I say.

"And GO MARESA!" Daddy adds.

His block letters are striped and polka-dotted, yours are filled with hearts, mine are lamely speckled. But it's a handsome banner. We hang it above the living room window. Then Daddy brings out your boom box. "Back-to-school dance party!" Oh, Daddy, get a load of that nerdy twist.

There's a moment when we're all swaying. Hugging. You, Little One, in the middle. Then me in the middle. Then you, Daddy, in the middle. Then me in the middle again. The famous singer who died that summer is wailing about purple rain, and Daddy and I are holding you between us, squeezing, and we sway like one three-headed body with our eyes closed.

Then the fast songs. Then it's *Soul Train* to insane asylum in 15.2 minutes.

"More!" you're saying. "More!"

"Maresa, it's time to calm down a little, honey."

"Maresa, don't kick."

"Maresa, don't hit."

"Maresa, look, we're just trying to get you to —"
"STOP *HURTING* ME!"

When the screaming and the scratching and the crazed eyes
are over and your bedroom light is out, I return to the dishes.
Thanks be to God for the sound of running water; I'll never
complain about the dishes. If only the Post-it notes didn't stare
back at me. DIRTY. CLEAN. The handwriting large and com-
manding and crude. *We have to get that couples counseling,* I think.
He can't treat me like this, I think. So I head back to Daddy in
our bedroom, intending to tell him I cannot abide Post-it notes
over the sink, but on the short walk across our tiny house I'm
thinking, too, of how *he* wanted the dance party, how I *knew*
you'd get all worked up and difficult and so I *didn't* want the
dance party, and when I walk into the bedroom, what comes out
of my mouth is "You know, I warned you about the dance party."
   "Is that really necessary?" he says. "I feel lousy enough."
   But I do it again.
   "Well, I'm just saying, I *did* warn you."

Do we shout in this family?
   Raised voices, I'd call them.

It's astonishing how one minute you're the NASCAR driver on
meth, Little One, and then the next you're stone-cold asleep in
your bed.
   I watch you in the dark. Then you rustle awake. "*What,*
Mommy?"
   I cross the shadows to your bed. "Just, I love you," I say.
   "I know."

"Oh. Well, then, I'm glad you know. I'm sorry I got so mad."

The smell of you in the dark—do I imagine this loamy sweetness?

"Do you still love *me*?"

"Of course," you say.

The human olfactory system is not so different from that of goats and guinea pigs, I'll later learn, as crucial to avoiding predators as to finding the right mate. I've always loved Sebastian's salty smell, too.

"Mommy," you say. "It's a triangle, remember? You need to tell Daddy you're sorry."

Happily, the next day is not the first day of school. Happily, Daddy took my advice and held the dance party *two* days before school, just in case you got out of hand.

So you sleep in, and I pull up the tomato plants. No sense watering them if they won't bear any more fruit this year. Daddy is eyeing the eggplant, promising.

I walk up behind him as he waters. Almost speak, stop. One and a half months since we told the workers we wanted to hold off on finalizing. I riffled through my pocket calendar last night and saw how the weeks have ticked by, and I thought about saying something to Daddy, but then I decided I'd better not. Not yet.

He doesn't tend to tell me he loves you. These days, if I ask, he says that should go without saying. But sometimes when we mess things up—forget to register you for gymnastics camp, promise a playdate that gets canceled—he does say, "I feel terrible letting her down."

That night at sunset, Daddy's the one who turns to me. Speaks without prompting as he sets down the hose. Says plainly, "I think we ought to get rolling on finalizing."

Fifteen

WE'D THOUGHT ALL we needed to do was snap our fingers and file the paperwork, call up surfer dude and get a court date.

"Just a heads-up," he says. "I'm hearing from other workers it's taking a little longer than usual lately to get the state to sign off."

I know limbo. All those years ago when I got flipped out about following Max to San Francisco unless we were engaged. He wouldn't give me a ring, understandably. "There's only two kinds of relationships," he said, stroking my hair. "You've either got your exit strategy or you're in together-forever mode. And I'm not looking for an exit strategy."

I spun that statement round and round in my brain, but couldn't get the double negative to equal a positive. Plenty of other men had told me, in high school and in college, that they didn't have an exit strategy. Plenty of men who ultimately decided I was too much.

After we moved to San Francisco, I'd be all lovey-dovey to Max for a few days and then: holy terror. So when you're all cuddles,

Little One, I know to brace for a day of hell that will follow. I remember the fallout from indulging an interlude of trust. Out of nowhere, in floods the dread. The vigilance. Max going out for a drink with a friend without me. I wouldn't make plans of my own. I'd just wait for him at the door.

Oh, the beginnings of the fights were always small. He hadn't come home early enough, hadn't called often enough. Tiffs. He always knew where I was taking things, though. Two a.m., three: "YOU DON'T EVEN LOVE ME! WELL, IF YOU *LOVE* ME, WHY DON'T YOU *MARRY* ME?!"

We went to a therapist together, on Lombard. There was a deep-dish-pizza place across the street, and afterward we'd go share the meat combo even though we'd lost our appetite.

"Max, you *seem* awfully committed," the therapist had said, glancing at me.

We looked at rings. But he didn't buy.

And then we moved in together again. An Edwardian across the street from the no-kill shelter. "Maybe-engaged," we called what we were doing. I'd begun my memoir about my father and the night of the blood, so I wrote at home in between stints of walking the dogs. I saw people come in and fall in love with pit bulls and Lab-terriers. I saw them take dogs home. I saw them bring dogs back.

The shelter's toughest case was named Rufus. I was the only volunteer they trusted to walk him. The only volunteer who could handle him. Story was, Rufus had been kept alone all day in a dirt yard with a barbed-wire fence. Which he jumped.

Which is how he lost his right eye. Just a pit of fur staring back at you.

Mild aggressions, the shelter staff had to warn. Rufus was a German shepherd. He snapped at everyone on the street. Beyond just ignoring the barking and snapping, the cure for this was incentivizing: a treat every time he walked past a stranger without an attack. You had to be sweet but firm. You had to pull him away the moment he reacted. But you also had to absolutely ignore the unwanted behavior. Which is hard when a sixty-pound creature in your charge is snarling like a rabid wolf.

That missing right eye. People came in and pitied Rufus when they first saw him in the crate. But they did a quick 180 when he snarled at them in the park.

I don't know if he ever got adopted, because I moved within the year. Needed to start clean. Stop torturing Max, stop torturing myself. Surely loneliness would be better than limbo. Max and I were done. Or so I thought.

Surfer dude is telling us to hang tight. "Paperwork's processing, I swear. Shouldn't be long now."

"Shit," I say when we hang up.

"I just hope she can hold on," Daddy says.

That last week before school started up again, before Daddy's commuting resumed, Grandma Annie came to stay with you so that Daddy and I could take a trip down to the Bay Area for "respite." We saw the latest Italian sensation in *La Traviata* —

glorious. Toured the new wing of the museum. Drank wine at sidewalk cafés, strategized. "Take Friday nights for your studio time," I told Daddy. "You need to make your work. You'll feel so much better." And for once he said I was right; he would do it.

"Sing for us, sweetie!" we said when we came home after our two nights away. "We missed your opera voice."

Silent treatment. You wouldn't look me in the eye. That was a very long night. The night you added new scars to my shoulder.

When at last you slept, I retreated to the room you're not supposed to enter. To my desk. A yellow Post-it. The handwriting so careful. I LOVE YOU MOM.

I pinned it above my desk, where it still breaks my heart now as I type this.

Sixteen

THAT SECOND GRADE ROCKS banner was a good idea. You seem to believe in the message, Little One. You wake up at 6 a.m. Say things so shocking that even now, as I type them, the words hardly seem real.

I can't wait to get to school!
I can't wait to see my classroom!
I can't wait to see my friends!

Back-to-School Night. Daddy and I sit front row. The teacher wears her hair in soft curls, like a 1940s actress. A silver heart on a chain around her neck. This is her thirtieth year teaching, she tells us, and she's never had a sweeter class. She fills us in on phonics, on comprehension benchmarks, on the memorization of math facts. "But my fundamental goal for the year," she says, "is to make sure all the kids feel loved and connected, to make sure they know they belong, to teach them how to pick themselves up."

I wouldn't believe those were her actual words now, if I hadn't taken notes.

⌒

Homework hour. "We have to use *very* good handwriting," you say as you fit your e's and a's between the lines. "Mrs. Morovian says so. She has high standards because she *cares.*"

Mrs. Morovian often emails us at nine o'clock at night.

I just wanted to let you know what a beautiful start Maresa has made in second grade. I absolutely LOVE her tenacity, resilience and outspokenness. I admire her intellect and her desire to do an excellent job. I also sense in her a very tender and tentative yearning for love and connection. I have her sitting in the front row, right by my desk, so that I can stay connected to her.

Sometimes, you tell me, Mrs. Morovian comes around while you're finishing a worksheet and scratches behind your ear.

"We're finalizing as soon as possible," I tell Mrs. Morovian at the parent-teacher conference.

"And starting her with a new therapist," Daddy adds.

The new therapist's website shows a picture of a salt-and-pepper-haired woman in jeans and boots. Her office is out on what she calls her ranch, fifteen miles from town, all rolling hills and benevolent oaks. The website includes pictures of her "assistants" — three horses, two cats, and a Chihuahua.

We have to stick to our guns, choosing this therapist. We have to nag Medi-Cal ourselves when the grey-crowned social worker tells us the insurance won't work, this can't be done. A month spent working the system, a new Medi-Cal card the prize. And then another six weeks before this therapist and her "assistants" have an opening.

⌒

I'm still thinking on the advice the psychiatrist gave me. "You may want to give her some more transitional objects. Something that's really special to you." But I can never find the right thing.

"No theme parks this time," I say to Grandma Annie. "She does best in nature."

So for fall break, to try again with your uncle, we drive to his house near the ocean. Eat spaghetti dinners with your one- and three-year-old cousins. Board a boat to an island with no electricity, no running water, just native foxes and miles of trails. You never tire on the hills; you'd go hours more if we didn't have to catch the boat back. But returning is the best part. A dolphin pod in the distance. The captain steers for it. And then hundreds of shining dolphins are speeding alongside the stern, and you hold your face in the sea spray, making friendly shrieks and shouting, "I'm speaking dolphin!" And this time my brother has no reproaches for me, thank God, though he does observe of your voice, "Christ, that girl's got a pair of lungs."

It's eight hours home, up the I-5. Daddy and I switch off with the driving, whoever's not behind the wheel sitting with you in the back seat as you read to us. The bathroom in the Bakersfield gas station isn't what we'd hoped. I buy you Red Vines to help you forget the graffitied walls and shit-splattered floor. Not until later does it occur to me that you probably saw many such bathrooms in your preschool years. Not until you get back in the car, jaw stiff, and say, "I wish you were adopting me tomorrow."

Soon, we say. So soon.

c

"I don't know what's going on with the state," surfer dude said. "They never take *this* long."

To break up the drive, we stop at Grandma Annie and Papa's. It's your birthday. We've made big plans. Chuck E. Cheese, which you've been asking us to take you to for months. You've told us you like to play the game where you aim at the rings and roll the ball, because the points become tickets you trade in for toys. We think this means you'll play Skee-Ball a bit, have pizza and cake a bit, play with other kids a bit. But as soon as we walk into the place, you ignore the giant talking mouse and the screaming kids and park yourself in front of a ramp. The moment the token drops and the balls clatter into the chute, you're throwing them rapid-fire, not stopping to aim. You remind me of the smoking zombie women I've seen in Reno pulling levers on the slot machines. Two hours you pass in this frenzied trance, whereupon you take your winning tickets to the prize counter and proceed to buy eight plastic whistles, ten plastic tops, fifteen Tootsie Rolls, and five Chuck E. Cheese stickers. Then hoist your bag of loot and say, "I did *all* that work for *this?*" Looking like you're going to cry. You give half the whistles and tops to strangers in the parking lot.

And yet, on the whole, the birthday celebration must be counted a success. When the grey-crowned social worker comes for her visit and asks how your birthday was, you do that thing where your eyes roll back maniacally as you cackle with pleasure.

We've put you in a community choir for kids five to eight. You stand between two redheaded twins and recite, "Stand up, feet apart, knees relaxed, and shoulders down. Hands and arms are at your sides, now we are ready to sing." You sing a song about Humpty Dumpty, you sing "All Things Bright and Beautiful," you learn *do re mi*. Pitch is easy for you, but the "hands and arms are at your sides" part presents a challenge. You poke the redheaded girls, make bunny ears behind their heads while they're listening to the cheerily rotund choir director.

"She won't let me use my opera voice," you explain.

It's a two-hour battle, the following week, to get you to go back. Look, it's over in forty-five minutes, we say. You made a commitment to the group, we say.

So you throw yourself on the floor, screaming. Then, when I say "Last chance! Come to choir *now* or no video time for *two* weeks," you tuck your hair behind your ears, wipe your nose, and pull yourself together.

You still poke the redheaded twins every two minutes, but the cheerily rotund director says, "It's okay. Kids this age are just learning, and some more than others."

I make a mental note to write her a love letter.

"It's all about patience," she says.

Mrs. Morovian's patience, too, is superhuman. We learn about it from the principal, when she calls me and Daddy in after school to tell us about your day. The principal is short and shrewd-eyed; I've seen her wither a child with one glance. "Well, your daughter had quite a scene today," she begins.

Apparently you were refusing to put away your colored pencils, and then, when Mrs. Morovian took them away, you stood up and started stamping the carpet in front of the cubbies and shouting "*No!*" And then you were rolling on the carpet and crying and then gasping so hard you were choking and then you were calling out "Help me!" while swatting Mrs. Morovian away. She sent the rest of the students into the neighboring teacher's classroom. Sat with you on the carpet for forty-five minutes until at last you stopped shrieking and choking. Told you to breathe. Got you sitting in your chair. Asked if you'd like to draw a picture for her. Said your drawing of a mermaid was very good; she could see how careful you were about shading. Told you that you were safe and loved, and asked if you were feeling better, before bringing the other children back in to continue the math lesson.

"She didn't want Maresa to feel singled out and punished for her panic," the principal says. "That woman is a saint, you know."

"She won't be able to do that *every* time," Daddy whispers to me.

We all thought this experience would create a bond between you and Mrs. Morovian, but alas, love is never that simple. You mimic her voice now when she's calling out class instructions. Say you won't stop walking on top of the playground wall unless she can explain to you *why* that's a rule. Rip a spelling test in half right in her face.

Maresa has a very special place in my heart and I feel grateful that I can create a space for her and a relationship with her where healing can take place. She is teaching me a lot about resilience, courage and trust. I feel blessed to have her in my class.

That's what the 9 p.m. emails still say.

It's an "hourly incentivizing system." You'll check in with the principal every morning. Carry around a card with smiley faces and frowny faces and an elaborate point system to earn prizes, like serving as crossing guard for the day. You'll check out with the principal every afternoon. They've seen it work very well with the Dillards' son, the principal says. I know the name. The Dillards worked through the same foster services agency. Tammy Dillard was one of the fost-adopt parents the grey-crowned social worker arranged for me to talk to during our home study, in the interest of realistic expectations. "It's much harder than we expected," Tammy Dillard told me a year ago. Which I took, then, as another pat on the back.

Wikipedia wisdom one might expect a woman who teaches creative writing to already know: *In writing and literature hubris is generally considered a "tragic flaw" and it is saved for the protagonist.*

One day the card is all frowny faces. "What happened?" I ask, as we sit down at the table to attempt homework.

"Ask Mrs. Morovian! Ask her why she hates me. Ask her why she *shoved* me!"

"Maresa, that's a very serious thing to say. Are you sure she didn't —"

"I saw it in her *eyes*, Mommy. She was walking past my desk and she went like *this* and she looked at me like *this.*"

"Maresa, she probably —"

"She's mean, Mommy! And *ugly.*"

⌒

I'm sorry, Little One, I'll never believe Mrs. Morovian shoved you. But that morning in the kitchen when you said, "One time, my birth mom's boyfriend? He grabbed my neck like this and he pulled me. With his hands on my neck. Off the GROUND. Like this."

That, I believe.

I take you to the kitchen store to pick out fancy jam for Mrs. Morovian. We write a card. *Thank you for teaching me*, you scrawl.

But you never change your tune about Mrs. Morovian.

"When are you adopting me?"

Soon, we say, soon. Hopefully next month.

"That's what you said *last* month."

"I promise you, I'm nagging the state every week" is all surfer dude can say.

Distraction tactics, that's all we've got left up our sleeves. *Tell us again what you want for Christmas!*

We drive to Grandma Annie and Papa's for Thanksgiving. Your uncle and aunt and your cousins meet us there. You scream a lot at bedtime, refuse to take baths or brush teeth. Your uncle and aunt and their kids stay outside in a motor home while we stay in the house's guest room, and your uncle and I have some good midnight chats. Not the smoothest of holidays, no, but to be honest, I hardly remember it.

What I do remember from that November is our first session with the new therapist, the one out in the country with the four-legged "assistants." How you fed the dappled gelding and the bay mare, petted the cat, played tug of war with the Chihuahua. How the new therapist said anything you shared there could be your secret, and how, when you didn't believe her, she pointed to the horizon and said, "No one can hear us out here. So go ahead, Maresa, scream!" And your scream echoed over the rolling hills. But there was something new in it. Something like freedom.

When the session was finished, the therapist held the dog's paw and waved bye and said, "We're all very pleased to meet you, Maresa, and I'd say we're off to a great start."

Daddy drove and I sat in the front seat on the way home, you in the back. The long stretch from the dirt road to the twisty paved one. We strained to hear the voices on the radio filling airtime, waiting for the election returns. The oak leaves yellow, the maple leaves red. The sunset burning a shade I'd call hope. "Our first woman president," Daddy said.

"Shhh!" I said. "Don't jinx it." But I was smiling.

You from the back seat: "So they're not going to build a wall?"

By the time we got home, it was dark. Daddy turned on the radio. The announcers' voices had changed. They were calling out states. Iowa. Ohio. Michigan. Dear God, Michigan. When they called Michigan, everything became present tense.

I place a hand on Daddy's heart.

"What's wrong?" you say in your pajamas. It's okay, honey, we say. We're in shock, we say.

You fall asleep. We tremble in the dark. The cat purring. "The animals don't know," Daddy says.

Daddy sitting on the edge of the bed with his head in his hands. Me kneeling with my face on his knees. "We've lost our country," Daddy says. "I don't — I don't even see how we carry on."

We have to, I say. For her. And never have I meant a word I have spoken more solemnly. "Whatever we do, we can't let her see us lose hope."

Three days after the election, surfer dude calls. "Ah, man, I'm sorry, guys. Apparently the state was backlogged and — sheesh. I've never seen a wait like that. But you're cleared now."

He says an envelope from the state is on the way, decreeing that the adoption may proceed.

"I hope it's in time," Daddy says.

But it wasn't.

Seventeen

OR MAYBE THE ADOPTION DELAY wasn't the cause. Maybe the gun would have gone off anyway. Maybe the holiday season was to blame. "Christmas can be very triggering." Hadn't the social workers warned us?

Triggers, the workers were always saying we should identify your triggers.

The thing about triggers: I didn't quite see the utility in looking for them. Bedtime was "triggering." Transitions were "triggering." Good luck arranging your life without bedtime or transitions.

So we'd stopped looking for triggers. And we'd stopped looking for signs. No more double rainbows. Months since we'd done the bald eagle kiss. But in retrospect, signs were there. Signs of what? Your fear, I suppose.

You started telling us we were "rude" again.
You started asking to play with your makeup.
You gave kids Indian burns at recess.

⌒

There are two recordings of you I can't bear to replay, Little One. The first is a video I made in the interest of memory. I made it a year ago, the day you came home with us for that first "pre-placement" visit, a small concession to sentimentality, I suppose. You're sitting at Daddy's keyboard. Wearing a green sweater Grandma Annie sent, too big, and a pink hat and scarf with huge grey tassels, which Daddy and I bought for you at JCPenney the day we gave you Mr. Fluffy Stuffy. You're sitting at the keyboard and your feet barely reach the floor and you're tiny in that big green sweater and that hat and that scarf. You watch your fingers press the keys, like a toddler learning to fit shapes inside a puzzle. Find the Vocals button. Press many keys at once. Your song a choir of angels.

I thought I'd watch that recording over and over, for years to come, but when I tried to play it back a year later, I couldn't stand it. I remembered what the woman from my memoir class had said. Ten years since she'd tried and failed to help that grandson.

Any ideas about the trigger? That's what the grey-crowned social worker asked, in the kitchen, after the policeman had left, on the December day in question.

I picked you up from school. Let's start there.

You wouldn't look me in the eye.

"Did you check out with the principal?" I asked. You wouldn't answer. Just then the principal herself walked over to the car on her short, muscled legs. And you withered in the back seat.

"Make sure you tell your mother what we talked about," the principal said with one eyebrow raised.

But you were silent for the two miles home. While I repeated, "Maresa, you have to tell me. Maresa, you have to talk."

That was a mistake, Little One. I wouldn't do it that way again.

And I wouldn't go straight to Daddy when we got home, wouldn't shut the bedroom door behind us.

I wouldn't walk out into the living room with Daddy saying, "Maresa, you *have* to tell us."

"I *HATE* YOU!"

Was that the first shot fired?

We stepped back. "If you're not going to talk," Daddy said after a moment, "you're going to lose a privilege." Walking into your bedroom as you clawed at his back, handing me your boom box, holding you off as I carried the boom box out of the house, locked it in the garage.

"YOU CAN'T *DO* THIS!" you were shrieking. "YOU'RE *KILLING* ME!"

That, too, was a mistake, I see now. Taking away your stereo. In the social workers' lingo: escalating.

This part isn't on the recording. And I never took notes. I didn't need to. It will forever stand among the sharpest moments in my memory. The tiny yellow leaves on the birch tree next to the back porch. The slam of the screen door.

"I know what I want for Christmas," you suddenly said in a totally different voice. A voice like a low burn.

What? we asked, confused.

"A baseball bat. So I can bash your heads in."

⌒

That's when I snatched my phone up from the kitchen counter and pushed the red button. The other recording file I'll never replay. Too afraid of what I'll hear in my voice.

Oh, you want to kill us, do you? Oh, and now you're miming how you'll smash our heads in. Yes, I'm recording. No, I won't turn it off. Go ahead, if you're going to keep acting it out like that, just say it. It's a serious thing, you know. To say you want to kill us.

THUD. THUD. THUD. THUD.
   You're kicking the wall in the hallway. Then you stop. Look at the photos on the wall. Grab one. The photo of you and Daddy in the silver frame.
   You look at it like you're staring down an insult. Then you throw it.

Daddy in the other room, calling the grey-crowned social worker. If anyone's in danger, call 911, she says.
   You're grabbing my arm. "I want to hurt you!" you're saying. It's all on the recording I'll never bring myself to play.
   "I'm going to *HURT* you!" You hold my arm, and you twist it, and I cry out for help.
   Daddy pulling you away.
   "He's CHOKING me! Daddy's choking me! Stop CHOK-ING me!"
   "He's *not* choking you, Maresa. That's *not* what's happening now. It happened before, when you were with your birth mom, but it's not happening now, we're trying to keep you safe, *no one's* choking you!"
   The knock on the door.

⌒

The way you snap to when the policeman walks in. Like a dog waiting for a command from its trainer. Like you've lived this scene before.

I've often imagined the scene at Brenda and Joe's, the night they called the seven-day notice for the workers to take you and your sister away. Your sister started it all, you said. Talking back. Hitting. And then Joe dragged your sister into the backyard in the dark. He threw your sister on the ground, you said.

"Blow out." That's the phrase I'll learn later, during my midnight internet searches. The social workers never used this phrase, but apparently it's standard lingo among former foster children. As in, *By eleven years old, I had blown out of five placements.*

"So what seems to be going on here?" the policeman at our front door asks. And we all stare at him as though God himself walked in.

"Okay, why don't you start by giving me a tour of your bedroom," he says. You lead him meekly around the corner of the hall, and he sits next to you on your bed. "So how long have you lived with this family?" he asks. "Seems to me you have a pretty nice bedroom."

I'm eavesdropping from the living room. When you were twisting my arm just ten minutes ago, you seemed enormous, a muscled attack dog, but when you come back into the living room, Little One, you're so tiny.

"Well, thank you for showing me your bedroom," the policeman says. "Keep up with that knitting, and hey, listen to your teacher in school, got it?"

The grey-crowned social worker has just arrived. She'll sit with us for a while, make sure you're steady.

"Looks like everything's under control here, then," the policeman says.

I want him to stay forever, but voices are coming over his walkie-talkie. Thank you, thank you, thank you, we say. "Anytime," he says. Closes the door behind him. And then we all stand there, silent.

So what was the trigger?

The next day we will learn from the principal what she'd wanted you to tell us: You'd given some of the other kids Indian burns again at recess. Hardly the worst thing you've had to fess up to.

My opinion: It doesn't matter so much *what* the trigger was, because you've got hidden anxieties in you — anxieties that will take months, years, to soothe, if ever they can be. And when those anxieties have to blow, you'll find a trigger, any trigger.

But the grey-crowned social worker who stands with me in the kitchen after the policeman has gone doesn't see things this way. She tells me again to find the trigger. Says there's a training I should go to on Thursday, taught by a woman who adopted a very abused, very violent toddler. "Wild Child," the training is titled. The girl's recovery was a miracle. They were even featured on CBS News. I cannot think of anything I want to do less in the wake of what just happened.

The grey-crowned worker says, "I think it will give you hope."

Eighteen

THE FOSTER MOM who raised the "wild child" made recordings, too. Because the social workers were telling her there must be something in her body language or her tone of voice that was making the girl flip out.

The girl had been sexually abused by her dad, who topped even that trauma by killing her baby sister in front of her eyes. She was four when she witnessed the murder. She was placed with a very experienced foster mom who had already adopted several former foster children but was still bewildered by this girl's responses. In the video, the foster mom is asking gently if she can help the girl put on her shoe, and the girl is screaming and clawing the air and then turning her hand on herself to claw her own face. The foster mom's other children look on.

Then, in the recording, the girl suddenly stops scratching at her cheeks and makes eye contact with the woman. The woman makes a little gasp. Says, "There, sweetie. I want to help you. This is why babies have parents, to help them. Will you let me help you?" And the girl nods yes.

"That was the moment," the foster mom says at the training.

⌒

You brought a bag of makeup with you when you moved from Auntie's. The first time you asked to play with it, Little One, back when you had been with us only a few weeks, I left you alone in your room with the lipstick and eye shadow. Came back expecting ruby lips and blue eyelids, remembering the fearsome thrill of playing with my mother's makeup at your age.

When I knocked and pushed open the door, you laughed and I gasped. Your face was gone. Black-rimmed lids, crusted mascara: a nightmare clown. Where did you learn how to do that? Then I realized I'd seen this face before. Your mother. On Facebook.

We noticed you tended to ask for makeup during your darker times. We gave it to you, occasionally. And you always laughed maniacally with that face that wasn't you.

You're asking for your makeup every day now.

"This will give us documentation," Daddy says when I confirm I've made an appointment with the psychiatrist's office. Just what we want to document, and for whom, we leave unanswered.

"When I feel like maybe I want to do the *wrong* thing, here's what I do," you announced to me months ago over breakfast. "I have a devil on one shoulder and an angel on the other. And I say, 'Inky binky bonky, Daddy bought a donkey. Donkey died, Daddy cried, inky binky bonky. My mother told me to choose the very best one. *So. You. Are. Not. It!*'"

You finished pointing back and forth with the song, waited

for me to applaud your methodology. "So you don't really choose, then," I said.

"No! I *know* which one to start with so that I end *up* on the devil, and he's not it."

"Sounds complicated," I said.

The day of the attack, the day the policeman came, the principal had talked with you about choices. You'd told her you gave the kids Indian burns "because of all the bad stuff that happened to me with my mom."

To which the principal said you had a new mom now. A new opportunity. That you could make your own choices.

I was uncomfortable later, hearing of this speech, though I did not say so to the principal. Before he died, while my mother was still married to the sociopath stepfather, my dad used to tell me that as soon as I turned thirteen I could go to court for a custody hearing. My father was by that time remarried, to a woman who scared me even more than my stepfather, and several times when he'd picked me up for weekend visits he'd stunk of alcohol. "You get to go before the judge and tell him who you want to live with," my dad used to say. "Won't that be great?" How could I tell him I didn't want to live with him? I was only nine years old, but I developed stomach ulcers.

The one upside to my father's death was that I never had to make that choice.

Since the day of the policeman, you seem to want only the choices that aren't on the table, Little One. The shirt that hasn't hung in your closet in months because it's stained. The shortest pair of shorts on the first day of snow. Sandals in December.

None of us likes our choices now. Not me, not you, not Daddy.

My existentialist tendencies have never faded. I'm still drawn to complicated religious philosophy, even if I no longer have time for six-hundred-page tomes. I still love Kierkegaard. Kierkegaard, who reasoned that to stand before God, you choose the choice that must be chosen.

Or, if you fail to choose, said Kierkegaard: You fall into despair.

We sit together on the futon before school. I'm telling you that you can't wear shorts when it's thirty-seven degrees out, that I can't let you wear them because my job as a parent is to help you. "This is why children have parents, Maresa, to help them. Will you let me help you?"

You shake your head no.

"Do you want me to be your parent?"

"Of course I do! You're Mommy. You're the nicest mommy. You're not my *real* mommy but in some ways . . . you're more my mommy than my real mommy."

"But am I your parent?"

No.

"But that's what I want, Maresa. I want to be your parent. In order for this to work, you have to agree that I'm your parent."

"Well . . . you're *kind of* my parent."

"You have to agree that I'm one hundred percent your parent. Like I agree that you're one hundred percent my daughter. Actually, one hundred and *ten* percent my daughter."

You've squirmed to the edge of the futon. "You're *kind of* my parent."

"It doesn't work if you don't choose that I'm one hundred percent your parent."

"You're saying kids have to choose?"

"I'm saying kids *do* have choices, yes."

You whimper. Glare. Walk away.

That was not "the moment."

New tactic: total defeat.

Fine, I say — here's the stained, too-small shirt.

To which you say you've changed your mind, you don't want to wear it after all.

Fine, I say — wear the short-shorts.

And you come back out wearing pants.

Fine, I say, put on your sandals.

You reach for your boots.

I am saying "fine," but I am thinking something unsayable.

The next morning, when Daddy is still in San Francisco, teaching, I offer four choices of jackets. "I can't wear *any* of those!" you say. "And if you try to *make* me, I'll scream my lungs out."

Half a block past the crossing guard, you're rubbing your arms, teeth chattering. "I tried to get you to wear a coat," I say.

Another glare. "You should have forced me."

"I don't want us to spend the next ten years as her captors," I say to Daddy that night.

He spends an hour on the phone with surfer dude the next day. I watch him pace the living room, then hang up.

"He says it's all about relational identity. He's coming next week to meet in person. Just me and you."

I'm only teaching one class this quarter, so I spend my mornings at a café on Main Street, writing. The first hour and a half I spend with my journals open, getting down all the specifics of the latest struggles with you. Then I turn to my computer, to the memoir I've been trying to write for more than a year. About the years I lived alone in the studio apartment with the moonlight slanting through the kitchen window and the cat curled on the pillow. About the sound of my kitten heels across the hardwood floors. Such a crisp, clean sound through the quiet.

"So you actually *do* write. I saw you!" the mom who organized the first-grade Valentine's party says. "What are you typing away at?"

Escapist literature, I say.

There's an import store next to the café; I pass it every day. The walls draped with scarves from Africa and Bali, the tables loaded with carved stones you'd probably like.

The black kohl won't come off now, even after slathering half a jar of cold cream, and all around your eyes the skin looks bruised. "Why do I have to take it off?" you say. "This is how I *want* to look!"

"No more makeup," Daddy says.

And all through the days we say, "I love you!" Not feeling it. Which may or may not be the same as not meaning it.

And in your fleeting repentant moments, you say, "I love

you!" Seeming to feel it. Which may or may not be the same
as meaning it.

"Do you think she's even *capable* of really loving us?" I ask
Daddy at night.
  "I'm not sure she's capable of really loving anyone," he an-
swers.

What happened with the man who became my first husband:
After three years as his clingy, torturing girlfriend, I broke up
with him for good. Left the apartment across the street from
the dog shelter. Didn't give him my new phone number. I was
working as a newspaper reporter. Max sent the letters and the
flowers and the jewelry to my office. He was good at grand ges-
tures. Took me to a five-star restaurant. On the sidewalk, as I
plotted escape, he clutched my shoulders as though to shake
sense into me. He said our months apart had made him see.
Said he'd made his choice.
  And for the first time, seeing he really had chosen, I thought,
I'm not actually sure I love him.

Three years married. Oh, I could write a book about the reasons I had to leave. Real reasons — money, sex, politics, the
whole trifecta. For a year after our split I shared these reasons
with anyone who'd listen. And they'd say, "You're right, you had
to leave."
  But in fact I didn't leave Max, that's not how it went. He left
me. Came home from a week in Cartagena, resolved. The only
time he shouted. He had to, he told me later, because he hated
to hurt me but he knew it had to hurt. He'd rehearsed the part-
ing line during his vacation: "*Adiós!*"

⌒

For a year, I cried.

The second year, I attended every service of Holy Week. Knelt beneath the vaulted concrete of the cathedral. Collapsed, shuddering, in the front pew as the clergy stripped the altar and shrouded the cross. The kindly verger escorted me to the chapter house. I said I needed to give confession.

"He did the right thing, leaving me," I babbled to the priest, "the thing that had to be done. I mean, he loved me. He *loved* me! But the thing was — I didn't love *him*."

Sometimes after you've been screaming, Little One, I talk to Daddy about my past, shake my head in rue. "She's testing us," I say. "I know, because I used to scream just like that at Max. God, I was terrible. Night after night. *God*, I was rotten."

"I'm not sure you should feel so bad," Daddy says. "I mean, clearly he had his faults, too."

"But I'd harangue him for *hours* — over anything. 'You don't love me, you don't love me, you don't love me.' I scratched him once. I *drew blood*."

"He was a grown man. He chose to be with you."

That he did. Standing at the altar in his pinstripe suit, all nerves and happiness. While I walked down that church aisle thinking, *I guess I'm really going to do this.*

"I only thought I loved him because, well, I *needed* him. So I lied to myself. *God*, I was such a mess. And then I wrote the book, and after that I guess I didn't need him anymore. I was different."

"How were you different?"
"I was myself."
"Because you wrote the book?"
Daddy's right, of course. That's not all of it.

When Max and I first met, when we first fell in love, we read Nietzsche in bed together, all agreement: *Yes, God is dead!* I loved that Max had studied nihilism at the Sorbonne. We both saw Buddhist monks as quaint little novelties. As for Christianity — craziness, utterly impractical and entirely masochistic. Oh, we were so solid in those shared beliefs of ours.

But by the time Max proposed, I had wandered into the cathedral.

"GO *AWAY!*" you shout, following me from your bedroom to the kitchen, where I insert earplugs and do the dishes in an attempt to honor your wishes.

At which you stand in the kitchen doorway shouting, "HELP ME!" And then, when I turn off the water and remove an earplug, "NO! NO! GO AWAY!"

I'm sorry, Max.
Thinking, *karma.*

"I wouldn't say the meeting gave me hope, exactly," Daddy says. He's just back from the support group, where he met a woman who adopted her own son at age seven. The workers told her she had to be steadfast. Take the leap. It was all about unconditional love. Now her son is sixteen, just back from a treatment program for reactive attachment disorder in Utah. You're not supposed to put locks on the outside of kids' doors, but she has one on her son's. "Sometimes he's just too dangerous," she told Daddy. And so: a deadbolt.

"If we don't keep her — " Daddy flinches at his own words. "She'd have to transition schools again. I'm just trying to think of the difficulty for her. That maybe it's best to move her out during a break."

"Summer break?" I say, tantalized by a date that is at once real and unreal. "God, six more months of this?"

"Actually, I was thinking *now*. Christmas break."

Beautiful girl up on the stage, singing all those carols about hope and peace and love. Brave girl, chin up, dark eyes shining. On the last few bars you take the octave jump, release a beacon across the auditorium.

"We heard your opera voice," we tell you. "It was so beautiful!"

An angel announcing alpha and omega. A sound I can never unhear.

I'm sitting across the table from you in the early dark while Daddy is at the gym. I've just asked you for the fifth time to get in the bath. I've been thinking, *Please God.* I've been thinking, *Maybe we can make it, if just for tonight — just for once maybe she'll stop fighting and get into the damn bath.*

"You're rude!" you say. "You treat me like a slave!" Your face with those chewy cheeks and your teeth coming in so pretty and straight, and then: that hatred in your eyes — all day long and all through the nights now, that hatred in your eyes.

One of the books said never to break down in helplessness in front of the child, or the child will conclude that you aren't capable of staying above the situation. Daddy and I had agreed that we would never sob in front of you or drag you into our own hysterics.

But Daddy is gone, and the night is dark, and one moment I'm sitting up with perfect dignity, and the next I look at that hatred in your eyes and I just — break.

"*Mommy?*"

"I *want* to take care of you, Maresa, I really do — I *want* to take care of you." Doubled over with my head in my hands, shaking. You sink to your knees and start sobbing too, and now we're holding each other, both of us heaving. The smallness of the room, the darkness of that corner where we huddle, I can feel it even as I write this. I don't suppose I will ever fully escape the memory of that dark corner. "You just have to do what we say, Maresa. Okay? You have to stop *fighting* us. Please. Please! I *want* to take care of you!"

"Mommy, you're scaring me. *Mommy?* Do you need a glass of water? Maybe that's what you need. Here, Mommy."

.

What we need is a savior. And we've designated the psychiatrist. If we can just get you back to him. First available appointment, yes, we'll take it.

But then, the morning of: "No, it *can't* be canceled," I say into the phone. "You don't understand, we're supposed to be there in fifteen minutes, there must be a mistake."

It's the first Monday morning of Christmas break. You won't put on your shoes, so I've called County Behavioral Health to apologize that we'll be ten minutes late. Thinking as I dialed, *Isn't it a little strange that psychiatric services never called to confirm?*

"Well, it *is* strange," the woman on the phone is saying, "but there's no appointment for you here today. No — wait — let me see. Ohhhhh. *I'm* sorry. I don't know who you talked to in scheduling, but we never actually made your appointment. We can't, see. Are you still seeing a therapist at 333 Brock Lane?"

No, we have a new therapist, I say.

"It looks like the old one closed out your case."

I no longer knew to whom I was speaking. I had begun to talk to myself. "She'll always be my daughter," I was saying, not touching my coffee. Surfer dude. How I wished I could still think of him so lightly. He stared at me over his plastic cup of water. Daddy stared at me over his plastic cup of water. In a booth at the diner where we ordered no food.

"We can get you more help," he was saying. A new classification. Wraparound services. The far-off county would pay more. Even after finalizing. They'd send a child to Utah, if need be, down the road. They did it all the time.

But I was talking about marriage.

"I didn't love him," I was saying. "And I married him! Oh my God, I actually married him!"

The waitress set down the bill.

The men stared. They thought I was talking about myself. My own regrets. But I wasn't. I was talking about you, Maresa. About how I didn't want you to have to make the same mistake.

Nineteen

WE NEVER MADE IT to the end of your life book, Little One. So many blank pages. It stops with your birth father. The next section was supposed to be about your sister.

We had sent her letters. With drawings, and pictures of you with me and Daddy. She never wrote back.

The workers wanted us to keep in touch with her. We wanted to keep in touch with her. You wanted to keep in touch with her. We called. You squirmed on the floor as you shouted into the speakerphone, "How's it going, Jennifer?" and "I want to come visit!" Your sister was ten but her voice sounded thirty. She said, "Maresa, is your new mom in the room?" You said yes.

And before I could turn the speakerphone off, your sister said, "Maresa's mom, you should know that my sister and I have a difficult relationship. That's why we don't live together. Maybe someday we can be in touch. But I think it's best we don't see each other now."

"Her parents must have given her that script," surfer dude said. "They have a different, uh . . . parenting style."

We were told that they looked down on "touchy-feely." That they were the kind of family that goes deer hunting. Daddy and I wanted this visit for *our* sake, they were saying, not yours. Reportedly they believed it wouldn't be good for either of you girls — just something to make Daddy and me feel "holier than thou."

You bounced on your toes, though, Little One, when I said we had a date. Your sister's new parents declined to meet us halfway, but they'd meet. So, two days after surfer dude's visit, Daddy stays home grading while you and I drive three hours.

You wouldn't let me brush your hair that morning. You insisted on wearing all black.

At the gas station where we stop, you spin the rack of greeting cards around and around before choosing one with a picture of two kittens, nose to nose. *Jennifer,* you write, *I love you forever.*

It looks exactly like the roller rink Daddy and I took you to on that pre-placement visit, even though it's six hours south. And empty this time. Modesto. Apparently no one takes their kids roller-skating three days before Christmas in Modesto. The workers swore that Jennifer *did* want to see you. But the moment we spot her, next to the vending counter, I know: Jennifer wants nothing to do with you.

You know it, too.

"Come on, give her a hug," Jennifer's mother says briskly. Her hair is artfully streaked and falls to her waist in a style undoubtedly involving hot tools. Jennifer has brown hair to her waist in the same style.

Jennifer's mom laces up her daughter's skates. You bat my hands away, tear off with your laces flying. Only to come back after three staggering laps and let Jennifer's mom tie your skates.

I admire your sister's hair.

"I do it every morning," Jennifer's mom tells me. "I still pick out all her clothes, too." Her lips are glossy, her eyes lined, but tastefully. I watch you skate around the rink with your hair flaring. You insisted on teasing it to resemble a wild animal's. That was your choice.

"No judgments here," Jennifer's mother says. "I know what you're up against."

Shortly after you and Jennifer were separated, she tells me, she and her husband thought they might take you in, too. They had you come visit, to see how that might work.

"Maresa just crawled around crying like a cat, and she threw things, and then she kicked Jennifer in the stomach."

Oh, I say.

"Yeah. Jennifer's the fourth child we've taken in. And my husband used to work in group homes. So . . . we have a pretty good sense of what we can handle."

We watch you two play red-light green-light and hokey-pokey. Watch you go in circles. Separate circles.

"We have to leave in twenty minutes or so," Jennifer's mother says. "To be honest, we wouldn't be here at all except the workers made us. It wasn't me. Jennifer —"

"I'm sorry," I say.

We watch you fall as Jennifer glides past, and then her mother meets my eye.

"I can see it really is Jennifer's wish not to visit Maresa," I say, "and I respect that."

"I can't force her," Jennifer's mother says. "The things these girls saw."

"You have to understand — Jennifer was older," her mother says. "She understood more. She never wants to see her birth mother again. Of course it isn't healthy to pretend none of that ever happened. We've had Jennifer in therapy for two years. Still. You can't tell a kid how to cope."

"What did they see?" I ask quietly. "I can't tell from what Maresa shares. I mean, she says one of her mom's boyfriends made her sit facing the corner and bashed her head against the wall. And she says a different boyfriend choked her."

"Oh, that's not the half of it."

I can't address this to you, Little One. I need you to cover your ears. I don't think you should ever have to hear it. If ever you read any of this — and perhaps you never should — I want you to skip this. Part of me thinks I shouldn't write it at all. But I have to. You see, it changed me. And because it changed me, it changed *us*.

"Jennifer can't drink milk," Jennifer's mother says. "Because one night, one of the mother's boyfriends was jacking off in front of them. While cutting his penis with a knife. So now, when she sees milk, she remembers that and, well, she wants to throw up."

Not "abuse." Not "trauma."
  Specifics.

"Can I ask you . . ." I start. "Our worker told us you guys have been . . . holding off on finalizing."

What I'm not saying: *We thought you must be heartless for not finalizing as soon as you could.*

Jennifer's mom speaks with the calm of Athena. "It's a long road, this kind of adopting. You shouldn't do it until everyone's ready. Jennifer had some attitude issues, nothing major. You can't rush it. We'll get there."

She hugs me when we part, Jennifer's mother. "You have my number," she says.

I take a picture of you and your sister, and in it you're barely touching.

"My sister didn't smile," you say afterward in the car. We go to Denny's. When the food comes, you start to cry. You say you're crying because you stubbed your toe.

Twenty

THE NEXT DAY, at the café, I can't write about the years of blissful solitude and *click click clicking* across the moonlit apartment on kitten heels. I can't work up enough caring about life before you. I spend three hours making notes on you. On you and me and Daddy. On us.

Maybe that was our new beginning, or the start of it.

It's hard to choose, in the import store. So many different kinds of pretty carved things. A bin full of painted rocks from Guyana shaped like hearts. Each the size of a palm, each with an animal carved on top. I choose a yellow one with a giraffe. An orange one with an elephant. And a green one with a hippopotamus.

I know you will want to be the hippopotamus.

I'm not excited about buying these stones, to be honest. I picture finding them in a box of knickknacks set aside for a garage sale after you're gone. Thinking of the woman in my class who wrote about Sicilian cuisine. *Even though it was ten years ago, every time I think of Dylan—I just start crying.* Still, I buy the stones.

I fit them edge to edge on the kitchen table, heart tips touching. You're still out at a matinee with Grandma Elsie. Daddy looks at them like I've wasted money.

"I guess we said we'd try everything," he says equably.

You immediately pick up the hippo. "This is me!" you say.

"And that's Daddy," you say, pointing to the giraffe. "And that's you, Mommy," pointing to the elephant.

"Oh, of course, sweetie!" I say. And then, as though the idea is just occurring to me, "Let's each hold our rock in our palm, and then hold our hands together for grace."

Dear Heavenly Father, thank you for the flowers and for the birds and for the stars and for science and for animals and for the solar system and thank you for all the good things and thank you for all the bad things.

You begin, once again, to scream in the night. At three in the morning when you call out, bloodcurdling, we can't tell whether you're asleep or awake.

But I won't forget, now, those lines precise as razor blades on your thighs.

"You're safe now," I say, "you're safe," but still you kick and claw. Your eyes open but empty. "That's over now," I say, "no one will hurt you now," but you shake. Then Daddy reaches into the toy chest. "Fluffy Stuffy is here!" he says, and you grasp the bunny. Press it to your cheek. Pupils dilating as though you've come to.

⌒

I see her downtown, the wedding-ring-free gymnastics mom who always comes for pickup wearing a pantsuit. "So what's Maresa up to for Christmas break?" she asks. Something about the tilt of her chin tells me she's angling for childcare.

"Playdates." I never thought I would thrill to that word. Her girls are eight and eleven. We bake cookies together. We hike. You follow the eleven-year-old up her secret side trails and tiptoe across fallen logs.

And then it's Christmas. Daddy and I are still a bit numb at Christmas. But dutifully we carry out the holiday. We get you the iPod headphones. We get you the fake tattoos and the science kit. We stuff the stocking with chocolates and knitting supplies and watercolor palettes. On Christmas Day, to my great surprise, you want to wear your white sweater, the one that makes you look angelic. You ask how Santa's elves knew how to make iPod headphones, though you don't seem all that particular about the logic of our answer.

You seem actually happy.

"How was your Christmas?" the littlest old church lady asks me as you speed past her for the brownies.

Fun: *enjoyment, amusement, or lighthearted pleasure.*

I think of how you set out the milk for Santa so carefully. Remember hiking with the girls, your joy as you tiptoed across the fallen logs.

I say, "Our Christmas was really fun."

A year since you joined our family. We mark your height again on the doorframe, we cheer. "Three inches in a year and a half!"

We eat hoppin' John for New Year's Day. Black-eyed peas cooked southern style; Daddy mastered the recipe back when we lived in North Carolina. "The more peas you eat," he explains, "the better your luck for the year ahead." You take seconds.

School is about to start again.

That January, Daddy gives me a night off for meditation at the center down the street. I've been ruminating a lot on karma recently. About whether it's so insightful after all to think of loving Maresa as karmic punishment for how I tortured Max.

"Karma isn't punishment," the meditation teacher says. "It's just a description of cause and effect. And if your bad karma comes back to you, in this life or another, you could choose to see it as an opportunity, a chance to work through what you didn't before."

At dinner, at bedtime, I'm listening closely again to your prayers.

Thank you, God, for the good things and the bad things.

Dear God, help us help the people who need food.

After offering that prayer, you sit up very seriously and say, "Mommy, we need to help Lilly!" I hadn't realized she was still on your mind, since we don't have to pass her in the lobby of the cinderblock building anymore. You say you want to save up your allowance and give it to Lilly so that her mother can buy food. Daddy and I try to explain why giving money directly might not be a great idea. That it might make Lilly and her mom uncomfortable. We say we can donate to the hospitality

house, the food bank. You're agitated: "But what about Lilly! I
want to help Lilly!"

And suddenly I remember the day Daddy and I first took
you to the roller rink. How you stopped to help every fallen
kid.

The wooden crucifix carved in Ghana hangs above Daddy's
shoulder. He's stayed out late in his studio, "just experimenting," he says, with a mischief in his eyes that makes me feel light.
Outside, again, it's raining. We still can't believe the drought is
over, months into this winter of biblical rain.

"It would just be too damaging to move her, you know,"
Daddy says out of nowhere. "She would lose all faith in hu-
manity."

His pulse steady under my thumb. "So are you saying . . ."

"I guess we better run with this. Even though, I *know*, it's
more than we bargained for. But maybe we better run with it
and . . . hope for the best."

"You sound . . . less than ecstatic."

"I'm sorry. You know it's just . . ."

"Your Samuel Beckett side?"

For a minute of steady rain, he is silent. Then he pulls me to
his chest, and his heart pounds against my cheek, his frail heart
inside that frail chest. "She's a remarkable person," he says.

"She is," I say.

"She's our daughter."

I knew as the rain kept falling that our decision had been made.
Our prayer cast. No longer would we live in limbo. I was terrified. And I was hopeful.

⌒

Could you sense it?

You held my hand as we walked to school. You held my hand as we walked home.

I was so happy, I sang to you as we walked. The Beatles.

I think it was around this time that Daddy hung the portrait back up in our bedroom. My breasts, I still didn't like them. But there she was, that young woman with soft, lazy nipples. A few weeks passed with her on the wall before you crinkled your little nose and asked, "Is that you?"

"Once was," I said, not unhappily.

Out in the hall, next to the photos of your grandparents, I'd hung the portrait you drew of Daddy. The kind of art you can only make at age seven or eight, if you have the gift. You'd looked at him so closely. The full lips, the worried eyes. It's intense, being looked at that way. I remember the feeling from the way Daddy looked at me. I remember feeling loved.

Twenty-One

THE GREY-CROWNED SOCIAL WORKER was reassigned not long after the day of the policeman. The blonde bimple therapist is no longer at the agency; I'm not sure why. The Family Support Specialist realized she wasn't cut out for working with kids and moved away. I ran into her at the grocery store a few days before she left. She wore heels. She was friendly. I wished her well. She said, "I hope to God I never see another laminated chart."

The agency said we could work with its new Family Support Specialist. A peppy-voiced woman with an Irish last name and an autistic son. "Oh, Colin's done that, too," she says regularly. We still work with her. She helped us get "accommodations" with the school. Now you can go to your Quiet Room during class, anytime you need to, by making a secret hand sign. When you're having one of those mornings of waking up crying and not knowing why, we can take our time and hold you; no penalty for tardies.

⌒

For a few months we had a new local social worker to replace the grey-crowned one. She was twenty-five and knew nothing. We didn't care. We just made sure she got the court date. And asked her to take photos.

In the courtroom: Grandma Elsie and Grandpa Bob, Papa Tim and Grandma Annie. The judge was bearded and smiling. He showed me and Daddy where to sign. He said to you, "You don't have to sign, but there's a line here for your signature if you want to."

You didn't think twice. You reached for the pen. You signed your new name.

And then the judge gave you the special teddy bear he always gives newly adopted kids, the teddy bear you squeezed with those dimples winking.

We got a dog that same week.

It struck me only later how much that adoption day was like getting married to Daddy. Simple, really: just put on our best clothes and go down to the courthouse. Except, for our adoption day, we decided to follow up with a party. We went home from court and had cake and danced with Grandma Annie and Papa, and Grandma Elsie and Grandpa Bob, and the neighbors, and five or six of your second-grade friends. All *Soul Train* this time, no insane asylum. You invited the kids into your bedroom to paint watercolors, didn't glare when I peeked in and asked if you were having fun. You'd started calling lots of kids your friends. Often at the grocery store now you'll point down the aisle at some kid from your school and call out, "I see my *friend!*"

If that day felt easy, if it felt right, I think that's partly because of our drive home from the therapist's the week before. I was driving a little close to the edge of the road, which had no shoulder. You said, "I hate cliffs." Then you said, "I almost went over a cliff once. When my mom got arrested."

You'd told me about that night a few times, spoken of the policeman pushing your mother to the ground and handcuffing her while you sat on the edge of a cliff until another policeman saved you. I could never quite imagine the topography, but I never questioned you, either. I'm sure, in some reality beyond accurate gradients, you were sitting on the edge of a cliff.

We had reached the longer, straighter stretch of road now, passing the horses in their pastures.

"You know, sweetheart, about your birth mother," I said. Wondered if I should consult the therapist before saying this, decided, *to heck with it.* "Later, when the time is right, if you want to have a relationship with her, I will totally support that."

In the rearview mirror, your head was cocked like a pup's. "Really?"

"Well, when the time is right. After you get to be a kid. And when the time is right for your birth mom, too. But I will support that."

"I like that," you said.

We had just turned off the dirt road and onto the pavement, for the last leg home.

"It's not one or the other," I said. "You don't have to choose."

You held your finger in the air and you bobbed your ponytail and you spoke in your baby voice that meant you were nervous, or excited, or both.

"But I *do* choose!" you said. "I do! I choose you *both.*"

⌒

They grey-crowned worker had several times warned us that finalizing the adoption didn't make the issues disappear. That a lot of families wanted to believe going through with the adoption would change everything, and sometimes it did help, but we shouldn't expect miracles.

We finalized the adoption on a Thursday.

On Friday you went to school. Mrs. Morovian wrote a note on the back of your smiley-face point-system card.

Great day! Happy. Calm. Secure.

"Let's enjoy it while we can," Daddy said, waiting for the proverbial shoe.

Walking back up the drive beneath the pine trees with the dog, I hear voices from the bedroom window — and a rhythm: hand claps. A man's voice and a girl's together: "Tic tac toe, give me an x, give me an o, give me three in a row." Then, "Daddy got hit by a ME-TE-OR!" Giggles. "Line, line, number nine, spiders crawling up your spine!" Laughter.

All the way to the trees, your crazy, mixed-up laughter.

Oh, coming home to those hand claps. A different kind of bliss than *click click click*. But still: bliss.

One week. And then another. And another.

"She's still in such a good *mood*," Daddy said.

We finished reading *Heidi*. You got teary in the middle, when Fräulein Rottenmeier tried to turn everyone against the little orphan girl, but we all agreed we liked the happy ending.

We moved on to *Little House on the Prairie*.

⌒

I had you read aloud to me, the nights Daddy was out of town. Any book you wanted. And again you brought me that old standby, though I thought you'd aged out of it: *Little Miss Spider.*

> *Then Miss Spider smiled and held Betty fast.*
> *"I looked for my mom and I found you at last!"*
> *For finding your mother there's one certain test.*
> *You must look for the creature who loves you the best.*

"Mommy?" you said, and got up to fetch toilet paper for my nose. "Do you have allergies?"

When Daddy came back, we read your new book, the book surfer dude gave you at the courthouse: *Happy Adoption Day!*

It came with an inscription in messy handwriting: *Dear Maresa, I am honored and happy to have been a small part of your journey this far. Remember that life can be mysterious and paradoxical. You have always been a smart, talented, kind, and heartfelt girl. I cannot wait to see all the wonderful things you will do.*

The story of *Happy Adoption Day!* was simple, and the verse didn't exactly scan, but we liked the illustrations on the page that said:

> *Some parents come different, some come the same,*
> *But whether they're single or pairs*
> *You're never alone, you're always at home*
> *Whenever there's love we can share.*

The drawing depicted a number of different families coming to an adoption day party. One kid was coming with his single dad. One kid was coming with two mothers. You pointed to the man and the woman with a child. "That's us," you said.

Three persons. Strange that when each can be separate, the whole can be strong. At least that's how it seems to me, not that everyone would see it this way. For instance: the grey-crowned social worker. We invited her to the adoption day party, even though she wasn't our social worker anymore when we finalized, as a way of saying thank you. Her first question to me, as we stood beneath the birch tree watching you and your friends eat cake: "So, are you still working?"

I was genuinely perplexed. As it happens, I *was* working — more than ever. I had recently gotten a few new pieces published, and that had led to more teaching and editing. I had even taken on a third class. The ripple effect: I was making more money, so I was able to tell Daddy that he could teach one *less* class, go ahead and spend that time on his art. The ripple effect: He was making new drawings, had a show going up in the café downtown next month.

I've noticed, now, that he tends to let go of things — my dishwashing technique, say — when he has time to make his art.

All I said to the grey-crowned social worker, though, was "Why would you ask me that?" And left her to get another piece of cake.

Finalizing didn't change everything, of course it didn't. You still sped ahead, that day on our family hike when Daddy and I walked the dog and you rode your bicycle. You sped ahead and Daddy and I said to each other, "She's so trustworthy now, it's amazing." And then we rounded the curve, expecting to see you, and you were gone. Disappeared. For two blocks, the dog barking and us calling frantically, "Maresa! Maresa!" Imagining the worst. Telling each other, "Oh my God, we spoke too soon."

But then there you were at our back door. "What?" you said, with a hint of taunt in your little voice.

"You're in trouble," we said. But you weren't really.

Okay, maybe finalizing did change everything.

Which is not to deny the darkness. There will always be that. The important thing, I'm coming to think, is building the right structure to hold it.

That morning in the cathedral, a year and a half ago, when I knew only your picture and your name, I lingered with the young man hanging the photos of foster children beneath the stained-glass windows, paused over the artifacts of pain held in those glass cases. Then a woman came running across the stone floor. She wore long skirts and long hair, and they trailed behind her as she rushed for us. "You have to take that down!" she hissed. "That's sexual! It's offensive."

The young man tried to explain that the exhibition shared the experiences of foster children.

"I know," she said, "and it's offensive! I know about this stuff. I had my kids on the street. And as a Christian woman, I tell you, you *have* to take that down. People don't want to see that. It's *painful*."

The young man said he was sorry she was offended and directed her to write a comment card and drop it in the box. She huffed off. He and I met eyes. "I'm glad you're here," I said again. "Showing these things in this space says that it's holy."

I have spoken, sometimes, with regret. Because yes, if I could go back, I would do certain things differently. But perhaps I shouldn't think this way. A few months after finalizing, Daddy made a new friend, a newly hired adjunct teacher who also worked as a child psychologist. He was curious about your adoption. Daddy told him about the lows. He told him about the highs. He told the new friend we felt solid.

"They call that 'earning it,'" the man said. "You all passed through that together, that means something."

That essay written from the "we" perspective, about the boy who surfed on a plank of wood — I teach it pretty much every quarter now. It's only a page long, but the new students always find more in it than I'd ever noticed before. Last quarter a very smart reader, a retired librarian, pointed out "you" at the scene's climax, used twice, and to refer to two different people.

Others in that class argued that the pronouns didn't matter. Or rather, that they *did* matter, but the pronouns weren't the key to the point of view. What mattered, one particularly brilliant and sensitive mother argued, was the first line of the essay, the sweeping, from-on-high view of the scene's panorama. And: that curious first reference to the people in the story, not as "we" or "you" or "I," but as faces, faces looking up to the sky. What mattered, this student said, was establishing the view from above. A view that saw and held everything.

A girl on the carpet. A woman sitting with her. A thin, pale man. The girl thrashes. "I WANT MY MOM! I WANT MY MOM! I WANT MY MOM!" She curls into a ball. She is still screaming. But the woman is holding her. The man is holding

her. The dog is looking on. *Honey, to lose your mother . . .* , the
woman is saying. *There's no worse pain,* the man is saying.

So many other people are also in that room, unseen, and always will be.

The child cries. But she reaches. The family holds each other.
They hold tight.

That's one scene. But there's also this. A clearing in the ponderosa pines, the grass yellowed under June heat. A stick flies
across the field, a dog runs back and forth. "Let's do it again,
Mommy," the girl says, directing the woman on the baseball
bench to place one ankle atop the other knee with the bent
leg splayed. "Watch, Daddy!" she says, and wiggles headfirst
through the circle formed by the woman's legs, pulls her whole
body through, pops up, victorious. It's silly, what she's doing,
she likes that about it, likes the way the woman says, "You silly!"
and tousles her hair.

The dog, their dog, runs and barks.

"Watch, Daddy!" you call. "Watch!"

"Okay, sweetie, I'm watching!" you call back.

You and you and I. Whatever could ever be final between us?
Again and again, we will all be reborn.

Notes

Though this book is a work of fiction, most of the quotations from parenting books are drawn from published sources.

Passages on pages 32, 48, and 66 are drawn from *Wounded Children, Healing Homes: How Traumatized Children Impact Adoptive and Foster Families*, by Jayne Schooler, Betsy Keefer Smalley, and Timothy Callahan.

Passages on pages 32, 59, and 66 are drawn, with some abridgment, from *Beyond Consequences, Logic, and Control: A Love-Based Approach to Helping Attachment-Challenged Children with Severe Behaviors*, by Heather T. Forbes and B. Bryan Post.

Passages on pages 84–85 and 90 are drawn from *Attaching in Adoption: Practical Tools for Today's Parents*, by Deborah D. Gray.

The (excellently informative) book alluded to on page 60 is *The Body Keeps the Score: Brain, Mind, and Body in the Healing of Trauma*, by Bessel van der Kolk, M.D.

A passage from *Happy Adoption Day!*, by John McCutcheon and Julie Paschkis, is quoted on page 191.

Passages from *Little Miss Spider*, by David Kirk, are quoted on pages 37, 56, 64, and 191.

The quote from Raymond Carver on page 44 is drawn from his essay "Fires," reprinted in *Call If You Need Me: The Uncollected Fiction and Other Prose.*

The quote about paranoia on page 57 is drawn from www.mentalhealthamerica.net/conditions/paranoia-and-delusional-disorders (accessed March 20, 2018).

The quote about atrial septal defect and life expectancy on page 135 is drawn from https://www.ncbi.nlm.nih.gov/pubmed/1921234 (accessed March 20, 2018).

Acknowledgments

With overbrimming thanks to Lexi Wangler, for believing in this book and bringing it to fullness, and to Rob McQuilkin for championing it sensitively and expertly. Rob and Lexi, you are my double-agent dream come true. All gratitude to Helen Atsma, for understanding this book even better than I do and editing it with such care. Special thanks, too, to Laurence Cooper, who belongs in the manuscript editors' Hall of Fame.

I am gratefully indebted to my early readers, Ben Preston, Dimitri Keriotis, and Sands Hall, and to Frances Stroh, for being there through highs and lows. Marilyn Abildskov, thank you for your literary friendship. Thank you Jenni Ferrari-Adler, for the conversation that catalyzed this book. Thank you Sarah Erickson, for sending all the best reading. Elizabeth Bernstein, simply thank you.

Thank you to the MacDowell Colony for the gifts of time, solitude, and moral support. Thank you to the San Francisco Writers' Grotto for camaraderie and practical advice, and to the staff of Stanford Continuing Studies, particularly Scott Hutchins and Malena Watrous, as well as the continuing studies students who taught me so much in their insightful discussions of our readings. Thank you, too, to the faculty and students of the MFA program at St. Mary's College of California, for the environment of caring and curiosity during the semester I served as visiting writer. Thank you to the Community of Writers at Squaw Valley and to Janis Cooke Newman and Lit Camp.

I owe so much to the Program for Writers at Warren Wilson College, for converting me to writing as a life of suitable silence before mystery, and faith in particulars. Immense thanks to Frederick Reiken for his unflagging mentorship. Thank you, Laura Hendrie, for telling me I was judgmental.

I am thankful to my mother, Aleta, for saying I should write, no matter what. Thank you to my husband and daughter for supporting my need for writing time, and bearing with me through the accompanying financial uncertainty.

I am grateful to Pat and Rita at Java John's for a clean table and free refills. I also want to thank Charles (Tad) Friend, the long-ago Oakland landlord who, when I told him I needed to pay the rent late, said I should go ahead and take a free month's rent, because he wanted to support a writer. Nine hundred dollars that kept me writing. There are many more people like Charles Friend I should thank, but the acknowledgments would stretch longer than the novel. I hope these generous people will forgive me for thanking them in person and in my heart.

About the Author

Rachel Howard earned her MFA in fiction from Warren Wilson College and is the author of a memoir, *The Lost Night*. She is the recipient of a MacDowell Colony fellowship, and her fiction, essays, and dance criticism have appeared in the *San Francisco Chronicle*, *ZYZZYVA*, the *New York Times*, the *Los Angeles Review of Books*, *Waxwing*, and elsewhere. She lives in Nevada City, California.